A FAMILY AFFAIR

Denise Richards

A KISMET® Romance

METEOR PUBLISHING CORPORATION
Bensalem, Pennsylvania

To Bobbi and Duane for beating the odds.

To Steven, Linnie, and Sam for proving
it can be done.

To Mom, for everything.

DENISE RICHARDS

Being raised in the wide, open spaces of the Texas
Panhandle gave Denise lots of room to use her over-
active imagination. Luckily, writing gives her a legiti-
mate excuse for inventing stories with happy endings.
She now resides in Shamrock, Texas, with her husband and two sons and whenever she feels the need
for inspiration, Denise heads for the city park and
rubs the Blarney Stone.

Other books by Denise Richards:

ONE

"You're what?" Marla asked in muffled surprise, conscious of the people seated at the next table. Surely her mother had not just announced in the middle of a crowded ski lodge that she was *pregnant*.

"Isn't it wonderful?" Josie Crandall reached a delicate hand across the table to grab her daughter's for a squeeze.

Marla returned the pressure of her mother's fingers, but *wonderful* was not the exact word racing through her mind at that particular moment. *Impossible* was a good choice. *Insane* a better one. "Are you sure?"

Josie nodded vigorously, her green eyes shining. "It's been two months since I had my . . . well, you know."

Marla's mind raced with the implication. Was it possible? "Mother, I don't want to hurt your feelings, but it isn't unusual for menopause to begin at your age."

"Oh, I know that." Josie dismissed Marla's suggestion with a wave of her hand. "But we've been trying so hard, I just know I'm pregnant."

"We!" Marla cried, completely forgetting the close

proximity of the other diners. She was so flabbergasted by the fact her mother was claiming to be pregnant that she had forgotten there was a man involved.

"Of course, *we*." Josie grinned. "I realize you think I'm a wonder woman, but this feat did require a little help."

"Mother!" Marla whispered fiercely, reining in her desire to reach over and shake the petite blonde sitting across from her. "This is nothing to joke about. Do you have any idea of what you have done?"

"Marla, I am a grown woman, not some sixteen-year-old," Josie admonished. "I knew you would be upset by the news, but I didn't expect you to become hysterical."

"I am never hysterical." Marla pressed her fingertips to her temples and grimaced against the pain already flaring behind her mahogany eyes. Her mother being involved with a man wasn't the problem. She had nudged her none-too-gently in that direction for years. A baby brother or sister was another story.

Her mother had to be *crazy* getting pregnant at her age, if she really *was* pregnant. There were a million things that could go wrong. Had they thought about Down's syndrome? Two A.M. feedings? Baby sitters?

Pregnant and unwed. It had been bad enough when Josie was sixteen, but at *forty-four!* "I'm just having a hard time taking all this in."

Josie's eyes softened as she gazed on her only child. "You'll get used to it. I can't wait for you to meet Aaron. He's such a doll."

"Where did you meet him?"

"Here." Josie glanced around the beautifully decorated room. "He owns the lodge."

Well, at least her mother hadn't taken up with some ski bum or gigolo. Not that she would be of much interest to fortune hunters. Josie Crandall had worked at a diner in town for the past fifteen years, and as long as she could afford the price of a lift ticket, she was happy.

"When's the wedding?"

"I don't know," Josie admitted, the light in her eyes dimming.

"You don't know!" Marla was incredulous. "He isn't already married, is he?"

"No!" Josie assured. "How could you think I would get involved with a married man."

"Frankly, Mother, I wouldn't put anything past you right now." Marla fluffed chestnut bangs out of her eyes and squared her shoulders. "Where do we find this wonderful man?"

"He's going to meet us in his office in a couple of hours." Josie rotated her wrist to eye the time on her bangle watch.

A couple of hours, Marla thought. *That's what you think, Mr. . . .*

"What did you say his name was?"

"Aaron Westbrook." Josie smiled a secret womanly smile. Marla thought she might be sick.

"Great, I've got time for one more run before we meet him." Marla grabbed her hat and gloves before her mother could protest. "I need a little time to sort all this out in my mind."

RED DEVIL. CAUTION.
EXPERIENCED SKIERS ONLY.

Marla glanced at the sign posted on the side of the gondola and shrugged. A challenge. Good, just what she needed.

A challenge, a broken leg, anything to stop her from thinking about her mother's newest surprise. She simply was not up to contemplating the implications of her

mother being pregnant. Not *just* pregnant, but enthusi-
astically so.

Marla glanced at her fellow passengers as they
boarded. Mainly young couples more interested in each
other than the beauty of the scenery.

Feeling incredibly alone, she was relieved when a
single man squeezed on just as the automatic doors
closed. Tall and broad-shouldered, he looked more than
capable of conquering the mountain. His ski clothes
were molded to his large frame, and Marla took the
time to enjoy the picture he made.

Why did skiers always insist on wearing those darned
mirrored sunglasses? She would like to know what
color his eyes were. Did he have bedroom eyes to go
with those high cheekbones and full lips?

A slight incline of his head acknowledged her attention and she flushed. How embarrassing to be caught
staring at a stranger like that. He would think she was
coming on to him. Even though the very thought was
ludicrous, Marla couldn't remember the last time she
had even been in the company of a man except for
business purposes.

Forcing her eyes from the man, she stared at the
snow-covered ground below her. Several skiers were
winding their way down the long incline from the extreme top of the mountain. She gasped when one
brightly clad daredevil shot over one of the moguls and
landed on his rear end.

"Serves him right," the man in the sunglasses
commented.

Marla started to turn around, but the press of people
in the gondola kept her back to the man. Instead, she
tilted her head up and back trying to get a better look
at him. "Why do you say that?"

"Too much speed, not enough control." His voice held a tenor of authority.

"How can you tell?" She couldn't have cared less about the unfortunate skier at that moment. She was much more interested in the subtle scent of the man pressed against her back.

"I make it my business to know," he answered, but Marla had completely forgotten the question.

"I've never skied Red Devil before."

"You should be careful." Even though the man was several inches taller than her five feet seven, his voice came from the vicinity of her ear. She suppressed a shiver as the skin on her neck prickled.

"I plan on taking it slow and easy." She had trouble getting the words out.

"That's usually the best way." His voice was an intimate caress.

They reached the top of the mountain, and the man automatically placed his arm across her midriff to guard her from the crush of skiers. "Crazy kids."

The lilt of his voice belied his words, and Marla smiled. He held out his hand and took her skis while she stepped from the car. "Thank you."

"No problem," he assured and laid the skis on the ground in front of her. She hesitated before reaching out and placing a hand on his shoulder for balance as he fit her boots into place.

She didn't realize she was massaging the powerful muscles beneath her hand until he raised those hidden eyes to hers, a faint smile curving the strong lips she had already enjoyed one fantasy about. "Be careful."

Embarrassed, she carefully sidestepped her way to the markers indicating where the groomed slope began and she studied the course before her. One glance at the deadly lumps of snow placed strategically on the mountainside and she wondered if she had indeed lost her mind.

She watched a couple from the gondola kiss farewell and set off down the mountain in a dual procession. Glancing at her watch, Marla realized she would have to get started or risk missing the meeting with Mr. Westbrook. The man made his way to stand next to her. "Well, I'm off."

"Would you like me to follow you?" he asked. "Since this is your first time."

"No!" She cringed at the thought of the man being witness to the numerous mistakes she was bound to make on her way down. "Please don't hold up on my account."

"It's more fun going down together," he urged. "Trust me."

Couldn't this man take a hint? "Okay, but if you get bored, please go on without me."

Nerves caused her to straighten her ski tips too sharply and immediately she began shooting down the hill. Her skis plowed through the powdery snow sending a fine spray around her. Several times she almost fell, but the man shouted a few words of advice and, miraculously, she remained upright.

She quickly revised her earlier deduction of the difficulty of the run and concentrated on making it to the bottom, not in record time, but intact. Her thighs and ankles screamed in protest with each turn. The sense of control she felt on the earlier runs vanished, to be replaced by a growing sensation of panic. She had lost her mind! She hoped the Ski Patrol was waiting with a stretcher.

Gravity and the sharp incline combined to catapult her down the mountain at an alarming rate. She gave serious consideration to falling but realized it would be the worst possible action to take. If she fell at this speed she would probably break her neck as she tumbled down the hill. "Help!"

"Slow down, you're losing control!" he shouted as she flew past him.

"I can't." She tried to stop her rapid progression by pressing the tips of her skis together, but as soon as she moved them inward, she could feel herself wobbling dangerously. The muscles in her legs were too worn out to control the skis.

The incline lessened as she reached the bottom of the run and she was able to slow down a little. She managed to lock her skis into a wedge position.

Just as she was regaining control she hit the hard-packed thoroughfare leading to the lodge. It was impossible to slow down on the icy ground.

"I can't stop!" she screamed to no one in particular.

"Wedge." She could hear him right behind her. "Turn . . . Fall down." He tried again.

Since wedging and turning were proving useless and she was within yards of the main flow of other skiers, she opted for falling. Even with the decrease in her speed she was still taking a chance, but it was better than crashing into some unsuspecting skier.

Leaning backward, her bottom landed squarely on the snow, while both legs shot out in directions God had not intended them to go. Thank goodness her skis snapped off.

Something was wrong! She fell down, she was supposed to stop. Instead she slid painfully along the hard-packed snow and into the racks of skis situated outside the lodge.

"I'm dead," she uttered, spitting snow out of her mouth.

"Lady, you okay?"

Marla opened her eyes and found her reflection in the four pairs of sunglasses staring down at her.

"Sure," she moaned as the boys helped her to her feet.

"You better learn how to stop before trying that much speed," one youth advised. He couldn't have been more than ten.

"Thanks, I'll remember that."

She leaned against the racks for a minute trying to catch her breath. The man from the gondola slid up next to her with the skis she had left several yards back up the mountain. "Did you break anything?"

Marla had been flexing her aching muscles and shook her head. "I don't think so. Did I hurt anyone?"

A deep chuckle vibrated through the man's massive chest. "No, but it's a wonder that you aren't in fifty pieces. What happened to *slow and easy*?"

"I thought I might enjoy fast and hard. Now if you'll excuse me, I have an appointment." She hurried off leaving the man holding her skis, but she had to get away. If there was anything more embarrassing than skiing on your bottom, it was having your words thrown back in your face.

Her legs screamed in pain as she made her way into the warmth of the lodge. It felt good to her wind-cooled cheeks and she naturally gravitated toward the huge fireplace on the opposite end of the room. Several couples lounged on the overstuffed leather couches and a few had taken up residence on the large woven rug in front of the roaring fire.

Marla removed her toboggan hat and fluffed her bangs with her fingertips. Smearing her chapped lips with some gloss, she debated the intelligence of what she was about to do. Confronting Aaron Westbrook alone could cause problems.

"I'd like to speak to mr. Westbrook. It's something of an emergency," she told the young man at the reception desk.

A blond hunk much better suited to the beaches of California than the mountains of New Mexico, he gave her a slow, thorough inspection. Taking in the delicate curves outlined by her jumper and the small amount of cleavage revealed by the open buttons of her undershirt, his smile told her he liked what he saw. "What was your name, ma'am?"

"Ms. Crandall." Marla decided it would be better if Mr. Westbrook was expecting Josie. That way she would catch him off guard. After making a quick call, the desk clerk pointed the way to the office and Marla hurriedly knocked on the door before she lost her nerve.

"Come in." The voice was commanding. She didn't hesitate.

The room was large and a bit imposing. Rich dark colors combined with natural woods to compose a sophisticated decor. It was the perfect setting for the man standing in front of the large window dominating the outside wall.

Only his silhouette was visible against the white backdrop of the snow-covered ground. The glare hurt her eyes, preventing her from getting a good look at him, but she had the sensation of having met him before. He seemed to be aware of her disadvantage and she felt like a germ under his microscope.

"Mr. Westbrook?" She squinted against the reflection and carefully walked across the room toward him. While his manners seemed to be lacking, hers were fully intact.

Stopping directly in front of him, she held out her hand. He hesitated only a moment before extending his own to envelop hers. Her eyes were still adjusting to the bright light, but she couldn't help but notice how he filled out the expensive designer sweater he wore over his skin tight ski pants.

When he spoke his voice was hard and clipped, not at all in keeping with the sensuous slant of his mouth. "Ms. Crandall, I would like to have a talk with you before my brother arrives."

Brother? "That's fine, what I have to say doesn't require an audience." Marla refused to be intimidated by his rudeness. "I have to tell you that I am simply appalled by this entire situation. I feel I have a right to know what your intentions are."

Her outburst must have startled him, because it took him several seconds to reply. "Intentions? As in, what do I intend to do about the wedding?"

"Exactly." Marla was relieved that he was at least planning to marry her mother.

"There won't be a wedding if I have anything to say about it," he growled, and strode quickly away from the windows to stand by the fireplace.

If Marla was shocked by his words, it was nothing compared to her reaction to the man himself. Tall, at least two inches over six feet, Aaron Westbrook was an imposing man. She could easily see why her mother had fallen for him even though he couldn't have been more than thirty-five.

Thick black hair cut so that it fell slightly past his collar and the perfect bone structure that decreed his Native American heritage. His onyx-black eyes glared down at her and his lips were drawn into a tight line so that it was impossible for her to tell if his mouth was as sexy as the rest of him. Sexy and mad as hell.

"What do you mean by that?" Marla asked once her brain regained control of her emotions. What was the matter with her? Imagine, fantasizing about the man her mother was in love with!

"I mean, I intend to do everything in my power to see that there is no marriage." He crossed his arms over his chest and she tried not to notice the way the fabric of his sweater stretched to accommodate the position.

"That's fine with me!" Marla refused to kowtow to this man and she stalked up to him, her fingernail punctuating the air under his nose. "My main concern right now is the baby."

For a split second those impenetrable black eyes widened in shock and Marla realized her mother hadn't told Aaron about the baby yet. Well, too bad. After witnessing this Neanderthal in action, there was no way on this earth she would let her mother marry him even if he were willing.

"I might have known there would be a child involved." The man's upper lips curled in disgust. "I believe it is customary for me to ask you to name your price."

Marla opened and closed her mouth three times searching for just the right phrase. Words failed her. There simply was not a vile enough description to be found in the English language.

"I should think fifty thousand would be more than adequate." He walked past her to his desk and extracted a check from the top drawer.

Marla was completely thrown off guard by his callousness. She had already given careful consideration to bashing his gorgeous face with the poker leaning next to the fireplace, but it would be a sin to scar such perfection.

"I advise you to take this, it won't be offered

again." He shoved his hands onto his hips and glared down at her. "Nor will it be upped."

Marla stared down at the bold slash of his writing. Angry tears blurred her vision. She slowly crumpled the paper in her left hand before slapping him with her right.

Caught unaware, the devastating blow was landed on completely relaxed muscles. "You little . . ."

"Don't think you've heard the last of me. I intend to make sure everyone in this town knows what a despicable man you are," Marla shrieked as he lunged for her, grabbing her wrist painfully. *Had she actually hit this man?* What was happening to her?

He hauled her up against him forcing the breath from her lungs. She could feel the heat of his skin through the thick knit of his sweater. Her palms registered the slight tremble of his muscles as her fingers splayed across his chest. She recognized the desire flaring in his eyes and was shocked that her body was responding in kind.

He stared at her for a brief, deliberating second before his lips descended on hers. Her mouth opened in astonishment and he took the opportunity to slide the tip of his tongue over her lower lip.

Marla could feel her teeth cutting into the delicate flesh of her lips as she pressed her mouth to his. She found herself welcoming his tongue with her own. In spite of all the arguments her logical mind was conjuring up, she slid her hands up his chest. Hearing him groan, she tightened her fingers in the silky black strands falling over his collar.

The kiss was one of anger and shocked surprise. Anger that she was kissing such a cold-hearted scoundrel and surprise that she could feel such passion from a single kiss. She pulled back slightly, meaning to remove herself from this man and her dangerous reaction to him. His teeth grabbed her lower lip and tugged her back toward him. She dove back into the kiss with an urgency that both excited and frightened her. Who would have thought something so wicked would feel so delicious?

"Marla!" Josie cried as she entered the room and saw her daughter pressed so urgently against this strange man.

"Eric!" The last thing Aaron had expected was to find his brother kissing his future stepdaughter.

"Mom!" Marla wheezed, staring from the couple in the doorway to the man still holding her. "Eric?"

"Marla?" Eric questioned, his black eyes fixed on his brother. They finally returned to settle on the delicate, confused face of the woman in his arms. "You aren't Josie Crandall?"

TWO

It took a moment for Marla to register that the man whose lips had just done unspeakable things to her insides was not Aaron Westbrook. *Thank goodness.* "I'm her daughter."

Eric pushed himself back from the woman. "I think there has been a misunderstanding."

If he thought he could pass all this off as a simple misunderstanding, he could think again! "Funny, you don't look stupid."

"Marla!" Her mother's shocked voice reminded her she was no longer alone with this man.

"Mother, you have no idea what went on here, so I suggest you stay out of it," Marla warned, her eyes never leaving Eric's.

"Eric, just what is going on?" Aaron asked.

Eric assessed the situation and came to the startling conclusion that he didn't have a clue. "I've just been having a chat with your future stepdaughter apparently."

"You weren't doing much talking that I could see."

Eric forced his eyes away from Marla's to meet the

skepticism in his brother's. "Aaron, you told me you were engaged to Josie Crandall. When I was informed that a Ms. Crandall wished to see me, I naturally assumed it was your fiancée."

"I think I see what happened. This is Marla Crandall, my soon-to-be stepdaughter," Aaron explained. "That still doesn't explain why you were kissing her."

Marla had finally been able to tear her eyes off Eric to study the man holding her mother. Although he was very nice looking, Aaron Westbrook possessed none of his brother's dynamic looks and confident manner. He also couldn't be a day over thirty.

She watched Eric's eyes and knew precisely when he came to the same realization. His eyes locked with hers, and in the blink of an eye they were united. There was still the matter of the fifty-thousand-dollar bribe that would hold them as enemies. But in the matter of her mother and his brother, they were a team.

"Mother, could I talk to you a moment?" Marla pulled her mother from Aaron's protective arms and led her to the opposite side of the room. "Have you lost your mind? He is at least fifteen years younger than you."

"He's thirty," Josie informed her.

"Okay, *fourteen* years. How could you have gotten involved with a man young enough to be your son." Marla stole a glance at the two men, who were apparently having the same conversation. The hard line of Eric's mouth clearly showed his displeasure.

Aaron flinched once or twice under the heated tongue lashing he was receiving from his older brother, but he held his ground. They appeared, on first glance, to be evenly matched, but on closer inspection, it was easy to determine Eric held not only the physical advantage but the verbal one as well.

"I already told you that we met here at the lodge," Josie explained, her eyes following Aaron. "I didn't intend to fall in love with him, Marla. That's something you don't have any control over—"

"Oh, hogwash." Marla interrupted, her hand slicing the air between them. "You most certainly do. Love doesn't just pop up and hit you over the head."

"How would you know?" Josie fired back. "To the best of my knowledge you have never been in love."

"That's because I'm not ready yet. When I decide the time is right, I'll find someone I'm compatible with and fall in love." Marla shot a quick glance toward the men. "I certainly won't be seduced by some *Casanova*."

Josie gasped and stepped back from her daughter. "Aaron did not seduce me. I am a grown woman and knew the game going in."

"Well, you didn't know it well enough to use birth control, did you?" Marla scoffed, aware her argument was unfair. After years of trying, unsuccessfully, her mother had every reason to believe she was, for all purposes, sterile. "Now look at the mess you're in."

Josie held up her hand to stop Marla's hurtful tirade. "That's enough. You may be twenty-seven years old and twice as smart as I am, but you have no right to speak to me like this. I did not, I repeat *not*, get pregnant by accident."

Marla reined in her temper. This wasn't helping matters any. She didn't want to hurt her mother, she just wanted what was best for her. "What do you mean?"

"I mean, this baby was planned," Josie explained. "I have known Aaron for over a year. The first time he asked me to marry him, I refused. I didn't think it would be fair for him to give up being a father. We finally decided we would get married if I could get pregnant. I've been seeing a specialist in Albuquerque for six months.''

"That's the craziest thing I've ever heard." Marla shook her head in disbelief.

"That's the craziest thing I've ever heard." Eric's voice echoed off the walls, his battle for control apparently lost.

"I'm sorry if you're upset, Eric, but I am marrying Josie and we are having a child." Aaron walked across the room, his black eyes softening as they landed on Josie. "We would like to have our families behind us, but we will be together nonetheless."

Josie turned from Marla into Aaron's arms and held her face up for his kiss. Marla was surprised how strange it felt to see her mother kissing a man. Not a young man, but *any* man. That couldn't be jealousy, could it?

She never considered herself a jealous person, but then she had never had to share her mother with anyone since her father died.

Aaron cupped her mother's face in his hand. "Are you all right, honey? Do you need to lie down?"

Marla felt that uncomfortable tightness in her chest again and realized it was indeed jealousy. For fifteen years, she had been responsible for taking care of her mom and now this man would be taking her place.

"I'm fine, Aaron." Josie snuggled against his chest and hugged him tightly.

"I know you don't understand, Marla, but I do love your mother and I—*we*—want this baby very much." Aaron smiled at her. "I hope with time you and that hard-headed brother of mine will at least come to terms with this. Maybe even be happy for us."

Marla wanted to snatch her mother out of his arms

and tell him to go away. She also wanted to wrap both of them in her arms and join in the love they shared.

Eric didn't say anything as Aaron and Josie left the room. He had made a fool of himself once today and it wasn't a feeling he enjoyed. "I would like to apologize."

"I should think you would." The softness in her voice belied the strong words.

Eric's lips tightened, and when his arms would have reached for the beautiful woman standing next to him, he crossed his arms over his chest. "You don't know my brother. He's very vulnerable where women are concerned. This isn't the first time he has been engaged."

"It isn't?" Marla was surprised to hear sincere concern in his voice. He didn't strike her as the type of man to be sensitive to the vulnerabilities of others unless it was in a business situation. There, she had no doubt, he would be more than aware of anything that might be to his advantage.

"No. I've been forced to extricate him out of two similar predicaments in the past. Both times the girls claimed to be pregnant."

Marla gasped and reached out to grab his arm, feeling the muscles bunch under the thick knit of his sweater. "You mean he has other children?"

Eric shook his head and gently removed her hand from his arm but didn't release it. It puzzled him how such a tiny hand could wreak havoc with his insides. "No, both times the women were lying. That's why I offered you the money."

"You thought I was the one your brother was engaged to." Marla glanced down at their hands. His fingers had entwined with hers in an easy, familiar manner and she quickly slid her hand from his. She rubbed her palm along her thigh to quell the tingling in her fingers.

Eric settled on the edge of his large oak desk and swung his leg over the edge. "Yes. I apologize for the misunderstanding but not for the offer."

"That's despicable." Marla paced back and forth in front of the fireplace in an effort to dispel her excess energy. She wondered if Tennessee Williams-had ever been in a situation like this. She certainly felt like a "cat on a hot tin roof."

"So you have said." He reached up to caress the cheek she had so recently branded with her palm. His full lips curved into a slight grin and the sight did irreparable damage to Marla's composure. The man was dangerous . . . S.E.X.Y.

"I'm afraid I don't possess a very trusting nature. I must tell you I was more surprised by the fact that you turned down the money than I was when the other women accepted it."

Marla didn't doubt the truth of his words. "That's sad."

Eric nodded in agreement, and his eyes held the weariness of a man who had faced too many years of deceit, greed, and prejudice. "Our time would be better spent concentrating on the happy couple rather than my jaded character."

Marla sat in the forest-green wing-back chair facing his desk. "What do you think we can do about it?"

Eric shrugged and leaned forward to rest an elbow on his knee. "I don't know, but I don't think this marriage is the right thing for my brother."

Marla quickly agreed. "It isn't right for my mother, either. She's my mother and I love her, but she isn't very practical when it comes to the real world."

"Neither is Aaron. He's an artist with the temperament to go with his talent. If I didn't handle the financial end, he would give his sculptures away.'' Eric indicated a stone carving resting on the mantel above the fireplace. It was a subtle shape depicting a horse and rider. Aaron's Apache heritage was indisputably engraved in the piece.

"I've seen his work.'' She had also seen the prices attached. If all of Aaron's work commanded the sky-high prices she had seen in the shops downtown, the financial end was substantial. She thought it best not to mention the new sculpture resting on her mother's bedside table.

"Southwestern art, in any form, has become extremely popular lately, especially those works created by Native Americans. Aaron's work is now being sold worldwide.'' Eric rose to shift the log in the fire and the oak log sent a shower of sparks onto the hearth. He stubbed his toe at one large cinder until the red glow had completely disappeared. "You can understand why I am skeptical about the women he sees.''

"I suppose so, but I promise you my mother could care less about money.'' Marla was forever scolding her about her finances.

"Most people without money make the same claim,'' he said without malice.

"I resent the implication.'' Her voice held none of the anger she was experiencing.

"I'm sure you do, but I didn't mean it personally.'' Eric watched Marla struggle for control of her temper. She had fascinated him from the moment she had stepped into his office. The only description he had been given of Josie Crandall had been Aaron's very prejudiced one.

He had envisioned the same type of woman with whom his brother was usually entangled—big, tall, buxom blondes. Marla Crandall was a far cry from the variety of woman he had expected. To be fair, so was her mother.

While Josie Crandall was an attractive woman, she paled in comparison to her daughter. Marla's bright-red ski jumper did little to hide her figure, and the color was echoed in her full lips. His hand reached up to stroke his cheek. Who would have thought such a delicate creature could pack such a wallop? His body tightened as he remembered how she had melted against him, how her lips had clung to his while he had helped himself to the sweetness of her mouth. "I'm afraid this romance has taken on a new twist. One I'm not familiar with."

"Oh?" Marla hadn't really heard what he had said. When he looked at her with those scorching black eyes, she had felt stripped naked for his personal inspection. Her nipples tightened when his gaze lingered on the open neck of her T-shirt and she felt as if he had touched her with more than those fathomless eyes. Her reaction to this man was an unknown entity and she didn't have the slightest idea how to deal with it.

She had always considered herself to be immune to that mythical chemistry so often touted as the panacea for loneliness. Not that she was lonely, of course. She expected to get married someday. But it would be a marriage based on mutual respect and common ideals, so she had no idea why she had succumbed to these hormonal fantasies not once but twice today.

"This is the first time Aaron has ever bucked me on anything." Eric remembered the determination in his brother's voice as he had argued with him.

"Mom usually bows to my wishes, too."

The phone rang and Eric returned to his desk to answer it. Marla tried not to notice how the material of his ski pants stretched across his well-muscled thighs as he sat on the edge of the desk. "I'll be right there."

Eric hung up the phone and placed his hands on his hips. "Something has come up. Could I call you later in the week so we can discuss this?"

Marla quickly wrote out her number and handed it to him. She tried to pretend it was fatigue that caused her hands to tremble as he took the card from her and not just the nearness of the man.

Eric picked her ski jacket off the back of her chair and held it up for her. "Don't worry, we'll come up with something."

"You've done a beautiful job renovating the lodge," she said as he walked her back toward the lounge. It seemed like a safe enough topic.

"I'm glad you like it." He placed his hand on the small of her back and guided her through the lunch crowd. "I might suggest you take a few lessons before trying Red Devil again."

Good grief, no wonder he seemed familiar. Eric had been the man in the gondola earlier. How humiliating!

THREE

"I don't think you should go!" Josie grumbled and fell back on Marla's bed.

"Mom, I've already told Eric I would meet him," Marla said, flicking her large brush over her cheeks trying for some semblance of cheekbones in her round face. "It's too late to back out now."

Josie mumbled something about her being a traitor and rolled over on the bed. Marla couldn't help the pang of sympathy she felt when she glanced at her mother's prone body huddled under the covers. Josie had gotten sick after supper last night and been forced to spend the night there.

She was still in bed when Marla got home from the office and hadn't moved except to protest Marla's meeting with Eric. Marla had considered cancelling the dinner meeting to stay home. They always took care of each other and it was hard for Marla to turn her back on her mother now. Still, she reminded herself, Josie wanted this pregnancy, and being sick was part of it.

Marla had called Dr. Reynolds this afternoon and he assured her that the queasy stomach, dizzy spells, and general irritability were perfectly normal. Knowing Marla's penchant for statistics, he quoted from several medical journals until she was satisfied her mother's behavior *was* normal.

"Why are you wearing that?" Josie asked, her head barely above the covers.

"What's wrong with this?" Marla glanced down at the pencil-slim black velvet skirt and matching cropped jacket. "He is taking me to the Avalon, not the Taco Hut."

She slid her red pumps out of their cubbyhole in the back of her closet and plucked the matching red earrings out of their drawer in her jewelry box.

She loved the way the red-and-black dress showed her figure to its best advantage. The skirt hit her just above the knee, making her legs appear longer than they actually were, and the peplum on the jacket balanced her slender hips with her larger bustline. It was the perfect outfit for business or pleasure.

She spritzed her hair until it spiked up in a punky yet sophisticated style and applied her make-up with a careful hand. A dab of her favorite perfume by Bob Mackie and she was ready to face any man. Unfortunately, Eric Westbrook wasn't just any man.

"It won't make any difference, you know."

Busy changing purses, Marla barely heard her mother. "What won't make a difference, Mom?"

"You and Eric can discuss us all you want, but it won't change the fact that Aaron and I are getting married." Sitting up in bed, Josie ran her fingers through her shoulder-length blond curls.

Marla caught her mother's reflection in the mirror; determination tilted her chin and brought a familiar spark to her eyes. "Mother," Marla sighed dramatically, blotting her red lips with a tissue. "We are just meeting to get to know one another better. He didn't say anything about you and Aaron when he called this afternoon.''

Josie threw off the covers, her eyes wide. ''This isn't a date!''

''No!'' Marla assured her. ''He just thought we should get to know each other. I'm sure he is planning to get together with you and Aaron as soon as you are feeling better.''

''Um hum,'' Josie murmured. ''He'll use anything to get his way.''

''Do you need anything before I leave?'' Marla asked, bending over to place her cheek against her mother's forehead to check for a temperature. None. Maybe Dr. Reynolds was right and the nausea was due to the pregnancy and not the flu. ''Are you feeling any better?''

''I'm fine, Marla.'' Josie grabbed Marla's hand when she would have walked away. ''I've been through this before, you know. I survived it with you and I'm sure I'll survive it with this little one.''

''Were you this sick with me?'' Marla had never given any thought to what her mother's first pregnancy had been like. She knew from the time she was very young that her parents were literally forced to marry. Her Granny Crandall relished in providing all the grisly details. She could still remember the harsh tones of Granny's voice as she told Marla how her father's life had been ruined. Granny never looked past the mistake to see the wonderful life Martin and Josie made for themselves. They might have had a difficult start, but they worked at their marriage. Marla had no doubt they would still be happily married if Martin hadn't died of a heart attack at the age of thirty.

''I think it was worse, but I really don't remember.''

Josie smiled at Marla's look of disbelief. "Really, it's one of nature's little quirks. Time really does heal all wounds."

Marla knew her mother was talking about more than just the pain of carrying and delivering a child, she was talking about the pain they had felt after her dad had died.

"Marla, do you think I'm being unfaithful to your dad by marrying Aaron?" Josie asked, pulling Marla down on the bed next to her.

Marla took a moment to think over her mother's question and really consider her feelings. Was that part of the reason she was so against this marriage? "I honestly don't know, Mom. I hadn't thought of it before."

Josie nodded. "I thought as much. Well, I want you to think about it. I'm much more interested in what you feel about my marrying Aaron than what you think about it."

"It's the same thing," Marla protested, rising to her feet.

"No, it isn't." Josie grabbed Marla's hand before she could move away. "You think with facts and statistics and logic. You feel with emotions and gut reactions. They are two separate entities that combine when you make a decision."

Not me, Marla thought, *I never allow my emotions to cloud the issue. Mistakes were much more likely to happen when decisions were made based on feelings. Mistakes like getting pregnant at seventeen and being called horrible names by your family. Mistakes like basing your happiness on another person only to have that person leave . . . or die.* "I'll think about it."

"That's all I ask." Josie smiled and glanced at the crystal clock resting on the nightstand. "You better hurry or you'll be late."

"I don't think Eric would appreciate that," Marla agreed and picked up her purse. "Call if you need me."

Where the heck was she? Eric glowered at the front door of the elegant restaurant as if he could make her materialize just by staring. He hated sitting alone. He always had the feeling everyone else was staring at him with pity. *Poor man, couldn't find a date.*

He leaned against the plush velvet back of his chair and held his watch up to the light. When he called this afternoon and suggested seven o'clock, she assured him that would give her plenty of time to go home and change. He never suspected Marla would be one of those women who took forever getting ready to go out.

He glanced at the front door again and back at his watch. If anyone around him should glance his way they would get the message that he was waiting for someone. It was a pitiful ploy and one he had never been forced to use before.

Finally, he thought as he watched Marla make her way across the restaurant. He stood as she neared the table and an apologetic smile curved his lips. "I was bad-mouthing you for being late, but I have to admit it was worth the wait."

Marla's cheeks matched the red of her earrings and she slid into the chair he pulled out for her. "Thank you."

"You're very welcome," Eric whispered against her ear as he slid her chair closer to the table.

Marla filled her lungs with his scent, and her stomach quivered as his hands settled on her shoulders for a split second before returning to his own seat.

She had begun to think her reaction to this man was a figment of her imagination. Instead, her response to him was even more unsettling than last week on the mountain. She would have to be on constant guard if she wanted to maintain any type of control. She didn't have any experience to draw on when it came to fending off unwanted desires. Especially not her own. "I'm sorry I'm late, but Mother wasn't feeling well."

"What's wrong?" He cursed the slight urgency in his question. Why would he care if something was wrong with Josie Crandall?

"Morning sickness." She busied herself with carefully unfolding her napkin and arranging it in her lap. She was uncomfortable discussing her mother with Eric. Maybe Josie had been right and she should have stayed home.

"But it isn't morning," Eric stated as if that should make a difference.

"That's what I said last week when all this started." Marla grinned and was rewarded with a twinkle in those midnight eyes. "I called the doctor and he explained it is very normal to feel ill all during the day. Mom has been trying all sorts of home remedies, none of which have helped in the least."

"Can't the doctor give her something?" Eric was clearly confused.

"He says it's better if she doesn't take anything for it." Marla shuddered at the thought of having to go through the same thing her mother was suffering just to have a child. And according to the doctor, there was more to come. "Some studies state that morning sickness is a sign of a healthy baby."

"Well, that's good news." Eric flipped open the menu the waiter had just handed him and studied it for a second. "I can recommend the trout amandine."

Marla quickly scanned the printed words before her, grateful for the time to chastise her wayward knee, which insisted on brushing against Eric's with alarming regularity.

Of course, he was seated right next to her instead of across the table where he was supposed to be. If he had taken the correct seat her legs wouldn't be in such close proximity to his, she wouldn't be forced to inhale his scent with every breath, and she wouldn't have to turn her head to see his eyes. Those inky black eyes had begun dissecting her the moment she stepped foot in the door.

"I'll have the Avalon salad." She calmly folded the large menu and placed it on the table across from her.

"Please don't feel like you have to eat light to impress me," Eric commented over the top of his menu, oblivious to the incredulous stare Marla shot in his direction. "I hate taking a woman to dinner only to have her pick at her food and mutter inane remarks about watching her weight. Please order something else."

Marla continued to stare at him for a second. "Mr. Westbrook, I'd like to make something perfectly clear to you. I ordered the salad because it is something that I like, although it also helps me to keep my weight down. I can also assure you I am not in the habit of making inane remarks about my weight, or any other matter."

Eric's eyebrows arched as he nodded his head in apology. "I didn't mean to upset you."

"What makes you think I'm upset?" Marla asked, consciously keeping her voice calm. "I was under the impression that we were here to discuss my mother and your brother, not my eating habits."

"That's not entirely true." Eric placed his menu on top of hers. Did she have any idea what that angry spark in her eyes did to a man? He didn't know about other men, but he found himself wondering if he would be able to bring out that same intensity in bed. "I did hope we might learn a little more about each other at the same time."

"I didn't mean to sound annoyed. It's been a trying week."

The waiter came for their order and Eric quickly informed the man of their choices, as well as ordering a suitable wine. Marla felt a tiny bit peeved he hadn't asked her opinion on the wine but knew it was a totally unreasonable feeling. What would she have told him if he had asked her? She knew absolutely nothing about wine other than you were supposed to drink red with meat and white with chicken.

"So tell me about your week," Eric urged when she lapsed into silence.

Marla had already shifted in her chair to face Eric before she realized her mistake. Her reaction to him had been unsettling enough when he had only taken up her peripheral vision. He was not a man to be taken head on. In any matter.

She clenched the white linen napkin in her lap and prayed her face didn't betray her agitation. *Get a grip, Marla.*

Eric had also turned to offer her his undivided attention. His left elbow rested on the edge of the table and she couldn't help but notice how the thin white material of his shirt had molded itself to the well-developed muscle beneath. She wondered if she would be able to feel the heat of his skin through the silk. What would his skin feel like? Would her fingers be able to trace the curves of those muscles?

Eric cleared his throat and swallowed the entire glass of wine the waiter placed in front of him. What was Marla thinking of that caused her eyes to burn with a desire so intense, it had practically scorched him from a foot away. He felt his bones turn as liquid as the molasses her eyes resembled.

"Your week?" he prompted when she only continued to stare at his . . . his what? Neck, arms, chest?

"Oh." Marla jerked her wandering eyes back to his face. "It's been really hectic."

"Marla . . ." Eric grinned. "You have to be the first woman I have ever known who has to be forced to talk. Getting a conversation out of you is like pulling teeth."

"Sorry, I just figured you were being polite."

"Not that you would know, but I am hardly ever polite." He nodded as the waiter came forward to replenish his drink. "If I ask about your week, it means I want to know. I have to listen to enough idle chatter at the lodge."

"Well, the market was like a yo-yo this week." She sighed and took a sip of the pinkish wine in front of her. She ran her tongue over her bottom lip to catch a tiny drop threatening to escape. She thought she heard Eric say something, but when she raised her eyebrows in question he motioned for her to continue. "Anytime you have a wildly fluctuating market you have the tempers that go along with it. Everyone at the office was more than ready for the market to close today. Hopefully next week will be calmer, give us some time to recover."

"Are you a broker?" If she licked her lips one more time he would not be held accountable for his actions.

"No, assistant," Marla informed him dryly. "That means I do all the work and my boss gets to take the clients to lunch."

Eric shook his head and took her hand, holding it openly on the table. "That's usually the way it works."

Marla shrugged her shoulders and glanced around at

the other diners. "I've thought about trying for my broker's license. I don't like the instability of it, but then I suppose nothing is very stable anymore."

"Such as?" His thumb traced a pattern on the soft skin of her hand. She really did have the nicest hands. Soft and capable of driving him crazy if he gave her the chance.

"The economy, world peace, jobs, marriage." She attempted to pull her hand from his, but he held tight.

Eric finally released her hand and leaned back in his chair. "Which brings us to the subject we are here to discuss. Very neatly done, Ms. Crandall."

Marla turned her head to smile at the waiter, who was grinding fresh black pepper onto her salad. "I decided my time was up. It's your turn."

Eric cut into his steak with relish and tried to ignore her suggestion. He didn't like talking about himself. He was much more comfortable knowing more about his opponents than they knew about him.

Opponent? When did he place Marla in that category? That was a label he normally reserved for those females intent on capturing him in their web. As far as he knew, Marla had no interest in him as anything other than an ally in the battle against the impossible pairing of her mother and his brother.

Oh, he knew she found him attractive, even desirable. He wasn't egotistical, just realistic. He knew the effect his looks and money had on women. He had recognized the look in her eyes before and known it for what it was. Desire of him as a male.

He also knew that had his face been captured in a photograph, that same look would have been etched on his face. He did want Marla. It didn't bother him, he had desired a great number of women in his lifetime, the only difference being, he knew lust was not synonymous with commitment and marriage.

"We're not as busy during the week, but things were picking up by the time I headed down the mountain tonight." He watched her mouth move as she chewed. "We'll be full up by tomorrow."

Marla was able to make the appropriate remarks during the rest of their dinner, but she was so acutely aware of his eyes on her that she couldn't finish her salad or the enormous slice of baked Alaska he ordered for dessert.

"Have you talked to Aaron lately?" she asked as the waiter poured their coffee.

"Not since Tuesday." He grimaced at the memory. "It wasn't pleasant, to say the least. He just won't listen to reason."

"Mom is the same way," Marla agreed, gladly embracing any subject not concerning the two of them together. "All she says is, they're in love, like that is all it takes."

"You don't think it is?" His voice clearly stated his surprise at her words.

"No!" she said with a firm shake of her head. "Do you?"

"No, but then it's different for me." Eric shrugged, the motion causing his hair to fall under the collar of his jacket.

"Because you're a man." She could feel the blood begin to pound in her ears at the implication. Why did it always have to come down to this? Couldn't they carry on a conversation without pointing out the fact that she was a woman and he was a man? Boy, was he a man!

"You have to admit it's different for a man." He

held out his hand to help her up, and she jerked from his grasp.

"I most certainly do not." She stood up and preceded him to the front of the restaurant to retrieve her coat. If Eric hadn't already paid for the meal, she would have taken great pleasure in flipping her credit card out. Different for a man, indeed!

The night air was freezing and her breath floated back in her face as she left the restaurant without waiting for him to hold open the door. It wasn't that she had anything against a man holding her door open, or paying for a meal. She thought it was nice, but she did resent them when they only did it because they doubted her capabilities.

"I didn't mean to upset you." Eric hurried after her.

Marla could tell by the sound of his voice that she was behaving exactly as he had expected a woman to react. She would show him, the overgrown macho toad! "Eric, I'm not upset. I only resent the insinuation that, as a woman, my decisions are based on emotions rather than facts."

"Is that what I implied?" His innocent tone bordered on sarcasm.

Marla sighed and leaned back against her car. "Eric, can we stop this little game you insist on playing. I understand you have certain misconceptions about me. I'm sure that I also harbor some about you. The cold truth is, we are not here to discuss whether or not I like my job or if you are capable of making an emotional decision. We are supposed to be figuring out a way to stop your brother from marrying my mother."

Eric placed his hands on either side of her, pinning her against the car. "I was under the impression your mother was trying to force my brother to marry her."

Marla reached up to rub her fingers against her temples. Was the man incapable of carrying on an intelligent conversation without having to snipe at everything she said? "Eric, at this point I don't think it matters. The fact is, they are planning to be married sometime within the next few weeks if we don't find a way to stop them."

"Frankly, right now I can't worry about stopping my brother," Eric stated, stepping so close that Marla automatically leaned back against the side of the car.

"I thought that was what this was all about?" Marla whispered, her eyes never faltering under his heated gaze.

"I thought it was, too." A pained expression flitted across his face. "It seems that I have another problem that has to be brought under control."

Another step and not a millimeter of space separated them. Even in the frigid air he caught a hint of her scent and he had an almost unfathomable need to bury his face in the bit of cleavage that had been tantalizing him all night.

Did she only apply perfume behind her ears or did she allow her finger to trail the scent down into the delectable valley of soft, warm femininity? Did she put it behind her knees where only a lover could discover it?

"Eric . . ." He stole the rest of her sentence with his lips and she never gave a second thought to asking him what his problem was.

She felt the fire that had simmered low in her abdomen all evening spread to heat even her half-frozen toes. The pressure of his lips increased slightly and his tongue slipped out to lave the fullness of her lower lip.

Straining against the building desire, she sought relief from the ache spiraling in her chest. His hands slid under the soft wool of her coat and brought her fully against the hardness of his chest. His need, it seemed, was as great as her own.

When the pain of his self-imposed torture finally became too much to bear, he made a conscious attempt not to grind his hips against hers. A move he hadn't used since high school. He lifted his lips from hers and, needing a few moments to compose himself, he pulled her face into the hollow of his neck. *This was not the chaste kiss he had planned.*

The cold air had reddened her cheeks and he reached up to finger the chilly skin. "It's a little cold to be standing out here having this discussion. Why don't we go back to your place?"

Said the spider to the fly, Marla thought. "Mom has been staying with me. I don't think she would like hearing what we have to say."

"Damn." Eric sighed. He couldn't ask her to drive up the mountain at this hour, and he didn't fancy having this *conversation* in public. "What about next week?"

Marla had managed to lower the rate of her breathing, but she still didn't like the quiver in her voice. "Eric, I think we've probably said everything we ought to say to each other."

Eric could feel her pulling away from him and frantically searched for some logical reason for them to meet again. Some reason besides his libido. "We still haven't decided what to do about this marriage."

"When?" She hadn't known she was going to accept his invitation until she opened her mouth.

"I'll call you." He quickly opened the door she had just unlocked and held it open until he made sure she was safely buckled in. He leaned into the car and placed a quick kiss on her startled lips.

"Eric, I agree we need to discuss Aaron and

Mother." Marla flipped on the ignition. "As for to-night's conversation . . .?"

"Yeah?" A small grin tugged at the corners of his mouth as he leaned down to stick his head in the window.

"I believe we've exhausted the subject." She tried not to feel sorry for herself. "Don't bring it up again."

"But . . ." Eric's words were lost in the air as Marla slammed her car into reverse and spun out of the parking space. "That's what you think, Ms. Marla Cran-dall. I have a great deal more I'd like to say on this particular topic. A great deal more."

FOUR

"You did *what?*" Marla drained the rest of her wine in a very unladylike gulp. "I don't believe it."

"Listen, I've been responsible for Aaron far too long to just cut him loose," Eric hurried to explain before Marla stabbed him with the steak knife. "He isn't thinking straight right now and really needs someone to put things into perspective."

"When?" Her voice broke slightly. "When did you send the contract?"

"I had my lawyer deliver it this afternoon." Eric winced, expecting to feel the full brunt of her anger. Instead, she buried her face in her hands and bowed her head. Immediately switching seats to place his arm around her shaking shoulders, he dug into his back pocket for a handkerchief. "Are you crying?"

"No," she sputtered before her laughter got the better of her.

"What's so danged funny?" He was incredulous. Where did she find humor in a premarital contract?

"We are." she stated finally, taking the forgotten cloth from his fingers and dabbing at the corners of her eyes. "Good grief, but we are arrogant."

"Woman," he growled, his eyebrows pulled together. "What are you talking about?"

"You sent my mother a prenuptial agreement to protect your brother, right?" Marla didn't wait for his confirmation. "And my mother sent your brother the same thing."

"I'm confused." Eric's voice left no doubt as to the limit of his patience.

"After what happened in your office, I knew Mother would have to prove she wasn't interested in Aaron's money or you wouldn't leave her alone. I had the lawyer in my building draw up a contract stating that Mom would leave the marriage with exactly what she brought into it. Of course, I did make provisions for the baby." Aside from the occasional giggle, her voice was calm. She could have been discussing the weather rather than her mother's future.

"And your mother agreed to this!" He couldn't believe it. His plan ruined! His perfect, well-thought-out scheme wasn't worth the paper it was written on. Snatching his handkerchief from her fingers, he crammed it into his pocket.

He hated it that Marla was right, but he was arrogant. It never occurred to him Josie Crandall would willingly give up her right to Aaron's money. As a matter of fact, he truly expected the contract to precipitate the end of this mismatched relationship. "Why would she do that?"

"Don't sound so suspicious." Marla shook her head at his stubbornness. "I told you she wasn't interested in money."

"Then what does she want?" Eric was still fumbling around in the mess of his own ego.

"Your brother apparently." Marla refused to back down under his glare. Instead of reacting in kind, she reached over and took his hand. "Look, I spent the better part of the week talking with Mom. I truly do not see how we can put a stop to this marriage. I'm not even sure we should try."

"Of course we should." Eric sat back in his chair, pulling his hand from hers. "I can't believe you have done an about-face on this."

"I haven't, not totally," Marla assured him. "I'm trying to look at all sides and come to an educated decision. I truly cannot see this marriage working, but there is the baby to consider."

"The baby will be taken care of." Eric motioned for the dessert cart and selected a large slice of strawberry cheesecake. Deftly cutting it in two equal slices, he shoved a fork at Marla. "Share with me."

Thanking him, she took a minuscule bite of the calorie-filled dessert. Eric had taken her to lunch three times the past week and each time he insisted she share his dessert. She knew how Gretel must have felt when the witch was fattening her up. "I'm talking about more than financially. What about PTA, Little League, homework?"

A slight reddish tinge emphasized Eric's high cheekbones and he concentrated on his dessert. "Naturally, Aaron will want to be part of his child's life. We Westbrooks have a great sense of family."

"And they won't have to go through the pain of a divorce," Marla whispered. Did he realize the audacity of their conversation? Would she want someone planning her life over cheesecake? No, never.

"Exactly." Eric jumped at her reasoning. "If we can make them see that this marriage doesn't stand a chance, then it will be much better for everyone in the long run. No doomed marriage, no messy divorce."

"I don't think we should get carried away," she

warned, exchanging her full plate for his empty one. "My mother can be pretty stubborn. We should simply show them how little they have in common, how difficult it will be to make this marriage work."

"You may be right." This time Eric was the one reaching for her hand. He had spent most of the evening securing Marla's aid in the potentially explosive situation and now that he had her firmly on his side, he could concentrate on exploring the feelings she aroused in him. "I hear there is a good band tonight." He nodded toward the adjoining nightclub. Why don't we check it out?"

Startled by the abrupt change of subject. Marla could only stare for a second. "Dancing?"

"We don't have to dance," Eric assured her, grabbing the check before she could reach it. "We've been pretty intense all night. It might help us to relax."

"Okay." Marla glanced around for the rest room. "Go find us a table and I'll be right back." She headed for the back of the restaurant. "And next time the check is mine."

Eric watched Marla weave her way through the crowded nightclub and his reaction was the same as it had been earlier—something akin to a teenage boy on his first date. He kept reminding himself that he had nothing in common with her, but somehow the message wasn't sinking in. *Face it, old man, you've got a serious case of lust.*

Dim lights combining with the smoky air cast an ethereal glow around her and he was reminded of an old black-and-white Dracula movie. The softly gathered silk of her royal-blue jumpsuit flowed around her with each step, molding itself to the temptation beneath before fluttering away. There was nothing remotely improper about the gathered crisscross neckline, but he couldn't help wondering about the secrets hidden by the loose silk. How difficult would it be for him to slide his hand through the vee to her . . . What? Willing flesh? *This was getting ridiculous.* Tonight was to secure Marla's help in the battle to stop his brother from making a tremendous mistake. *Nothing else.*

She was still several tables away when someone grabbed her arm, yanking her off balance. Eric came out of his chair and in the space of two strides was standing over the man ready to break his arm.

Marla's attention had been on Eric, and she wasn't prepared for the hand clasped around her arm. Instead of falling to the floor, she found herself ensconced on a male lap. "Bill!" Before she had time to catch her breath, Eric's hands were about her waist hauling her to his side. Sensing he would act first and ask questions later, Marla hurried to explain. "Eric, this is my *friend,* Bill Townsend." She placed a restraining hand on his arm. "Bill, this is Eric Westbrook, my . . ." Marla paused. *Her what? Date? Future stepuncle? Recurring fantasy?* "Friend, too," she finished lamely.

Tucking Marla to his side, Eric offered his hand. "Townsend."

"Good to meet you." Bill rose quickly and grasped Eric's hand. "I didn't mean to cause any trouble."

"No harm done." The smile on Eric's face didn't quite reach his eyes and Marla knew the two men were communicating in some silent male language.

Eric barely gave her time to say good-bye before half dragging her back to their table. She waited until he made himself comfortable. "Would you care to tell me what that was all about?"

Eric's eyebrows shot up. "I thought some drunk was manhandling you. I was trying to be chivalrous."

"If that's chivalry," Marla huffed, rolling her eyes, "I understand why it's dead. I can take care of myself, Sir Galahad."

"But you're with me." Eric pointed out in typical caveman fashion. "I can take care of you."

"Hasn't anyone informed you these are the 1990's. Macho went out twenty years ago." Marla silently chastised herself for making such a big deal out of his actions. He only acted with her best interest at heart, even if he had been rather like a bull in a china closet. She ran her hand over the vee of her jumpsuit, straightening the material. "Let's change the subject before we end up in another argument."

The quick tempo of the music segued into a slow ballad and Eric grabbed Marla's hand, pulling her behind him to the dance floor.

"Eric!" Marla hissed as he spun her into his arms. "What are you doing?"

"I think it's called dancing," he quipped, pulling her closer. "I realize it may be as outdated as chivalry, but I enjoy holding a woman when I dance. Humor me."

"All you had to do was ask," Marla mumbled against the crisp white fabric stretching across his chest, her ire fading quickly as he pressed her closer.

"Sorry." His voice held a ring of truth and she raised her eyes to his. "Would you like to dance?"

Marla bit the inside of her cheek to suppress the grin playing about her lips. It wouldn't do to let him off too easily. "Yes, thank you."

Eric's hand softly caressed her silk-covered back as he expertly led them around the floor. Despite the difference in their height, Marla matched her steps with his until they moved in unison. Sliding her hand along his shoulder, her fingers gently grazed the back of his neck.

The casual action sent a shock wave through him. Confused by his reaction to such a simple gesture, he scowled down at her. "Maybe this wasn't such a good idea," he grumbled, putting a few inches of space between them.

Marla's eyes opened at the abrupt change in his attitude. "Why not?"

"Because all I can think about is duplicating the action in a, shall we say, less vertical position," he said bluntly, needing to shock her into being her usual sensible self. It was enough that *his* hormones were running amuck.

Confronted with his honesty, she admitted to herself that her thought process was in sync with his. *Well, it was good to know they had something in common.* "Maybe we should sit down."

"Maybe we should leave," he decided and detoured her toward the front door. "Wait here while I warm up the car."

Marla opened her mouth to argue, but he was already dashing out into the freezing night. "I might as well give up," she murmured to herself. Eric had been getting his way far too long for her feeble attempts at enlightenment to make any difference. In a few weeks she wouldn't have to worry about him running roughshod over her anyway. The thought left her feeling oddly bereft.

Much to her dismay, she found herself becoming accustomed to his take-charge attitude. Despite her protests, she couldn't help the rush of pure femininity she experienced at his protection. Maybe it was selfish, but it was nice to have someone consider *her* needs for a change. *I could get used to this*, she thought, climbing into the warm car.

The low-slung black Corvette hugged the road as Eric negotiated another curve and Marla grabbed the door handle to keep from sliding out of the leather seat. She refused to glance at the speedometer. If they were going a hundred and twenty miles an hour, she didn't want to know.

Her attempts to draw him into conversation had been ineffective and, other than the soft jazz coming through the speakers, they had ridden in silence since leaving the nightclub. A sigh escaped her lips as he pulled into a parking space in front of her apartment building.

"That bad, huh?" He wrapped his hand around her upper arm as she reached for the handle. "I'm sorry."

Releasing the door, she turned to face him. Before she could utter a word, he reached over to cup her jaw in his hand and guide her lips to his. Touched by the gentleness of his action, Marla refused to contemplate the dangers of this kiss.

Slipping her fingers into the silky tangle of his hair, she opened her mouth under his and allowed him to work his magic. Erotic tingles coursed through her like electricity, and she had the sensation of sticking her tongue in a light socket. Caught off guard by the analogy, she giggled against his lips.

"Woman," he muttered on his way to the soft, fragrant flesh of her neck, "I'm not used to being laughed at."

"I'm sorry," she whispered, chuckling softly as he nipped at her ear lobe. "You do the strangest things to my thought pattern."

"I was hoping to stop it completely," he admitted, his breath a hot aphrodisiac in her ear.

"I have to go." There was no denying the panic in her voice.

"I'll walk you up," he offered, but she was already out of the door and halfway up the sidewalk. Her heels made quick little clips against the concrete and Eric shook his head as she bounded up the stairs. "Run, lady, there's nothing I like better than a good chase."

FIVE

"Marla, wait up." Bill Townsend dashed across the parking lot, his hand up in greeting.

"Crud," she mumbled through the welcoming smile on her lips. Chatting with Bill was the last thing she needed right now. Tossing her briefcase into the backseat of her car, she glanced at her watch. "I've only got a few minutes."

"Guess that means you're busy tonight." Pushing long fingers through his slightly rumpled hair, he leaned against the open car door. "I was hoping you might like to have a bite to eat. With me."

"Maybe some other time, Bill." Marla slid onto the frigid leather seat of her Chrysler LeBaron and started the engine. "I'm meeting Mother and I'm already late. I hate working on Saturdays."

"Could we have lunch next week?" There was a slight urgency underlying the simple request.

"Stop by my desk and we'll see how it goes." Quickly closing the door, she backed out of her parking space. Raising her hand in farewell, she sped across the almost deserted lot.

An uneasiness settled in her chest as she thought of dating Bill. When he joined the brokerage firm six months ago she had not been so immune to his golden good looks and boyish grin. He had factored into her dreams on more than one occasion. And why not? He was everything a modern woman could possibly hope for in a man. Educated and good-looking with a terrific sense of humor and a steady job. So why was she breaking at least five traffic laws racing up the mountain to see a man who would undoubtedly irritate her with his every word?

Although it was barely after five, the sun was already on the other side of the mountain by the time she reached the lodge. Saturday normally wasn't a working day, but the guys from head office were expected next week and since Monday was a holiday, she had agreed to give up part of her weekend.

She finally located her mother in the upper lounge snuggled in Aaron's arms and had to admit they made an attractive couple. Aaron's dark coloring was a perfect contrast to her mother's fairness. Looking like an angel in a snow-white sweater edged in metallic gold, Josie tipped her head back and smiled up at something Aaron said. No one around them seemed to be aware of their age difference. Or maybe they noticed and just didn't give a hoot.

"Mom, could we talk?" Marla settled on the floor at her mother's feet, tugging her skirt down over her knees.

Josie reached down to ruffle her hair. "That depends. Can you behave yourself?"

Marla nodded. Aaron offered to get her a cup of hot chocolate and she was impressed by his sensitivity. "Why didn't you call me and let me know you were moving in with Aaron? I got worried when I couldn't find you.''

"Aaron insisted I stay with him since I wasn't feeling well." Josie explained, her hand automatically straying to her stomach. "He likes to take care of me."

"*I* like taking care of you!" Marla jumped to her feet. She wasn't thrilled with her mother's pregnancy, but she prayed there weren't any complications. "Why didn't you stay at my place, I would have taken a few days off to take care of you. You didn't have to go to a stranger."

"I can understand that you're upset." Josie patted the couch next to her, and Marla reluctantly slid onto the soft leather. "Marla, Aaron isn't a stranger. He knows me better than anyone. We didn't do this to make your life miserable, you know. We did this to make our lives complete. I don't want to be alone for the rest of my life."

"You aren't alone," Marla protested. Alone! How could her mother say she was alone. Marla had always been there. After her father had died, Marla had practically forced Josie to find a job and get on with her life. When her mother needed to talk or had a problem, Marla had always seen that a solution was found.

"I am at night," Josie whispered, tears filling the clear green eyes pleading for understanding. "Every night there is a big empty space on the other side of my bed. Aaron fills it. He fills all the empty spaces in my life."

There was nothing Marla could say after that. Her logical, practical arguments were no competition for those tender, heartfelt words. She and Eric might not believe in the kind of love her mother shared with Aaron, but none of the arguments they had come up with during the week were any defense against it, either. She had to face the reality that her mother wasn't going to ask for her opinion on this decision, just her blessing.

Strangely enough, she was finding it harder and harder to find fault with her mother's choice of husband. Lately she was finding it hard to do anything but analyze her reactions to Eric.

"Aaron says you and Eric have spent several evenings together," Josie urged, and Marla thought over her meetings with Eric.

"We've been getting to know each other," Marla admitted. A delicate smile curved her lips. "I've never been around a man quite like him before. He acts like I'm totally incapable of taking care of myself."

"He certainly tries to take care of Aaron," Josie remarked, not trying to hide the bitterness she felt at having her life upset by Eric's paternal instincts.

"I didn't mean to upset you." Marla was surprised to see tears filling her mother's eyes. "Eric just has a very strong sense of responsibility. It's very hard for him to let go."

Josie held up her hand to stop Marla's explanation. "You can defend him all you want. It won't change a thing."

"When are you planning to get married?" Marla asked Aaron as he sat down next to them. She decided it was better to leave Eric out of the conversation entirely.

"As soon as I can convince that brother of mine your mother isn't Mata Hari reincarnated," Aaron grumbled, handing her a steaming cup of hot chocolate. "I couldn't believe he had that damned contract drawn up!"

"Honey, he's only looking after your best interests," Josie consoled, slipping her arm through his. "He doesn't realize that it isn't your money I'm after, it's your body."

"The feeling is mutual," Aaron assured, a faint blush tinting his cheeks at Josie's words. "Has he softened any?"

Marla saw the hope in his dark eyes so like Eric's and shook her head. "He still feels it would be a mistake."

"Because of my age," Josie said, and Marla couldn't disagree. "Do you feel the same way?"

Marla couldn't deny having reservations, but she also couldn't deny the love she witnessed between Aaron and her mother. "No, I've gotten past the age thing. Statistically it's more prudent for a woman to marry a younger man. From what I can tell, you and Aaron have a lot in common, and then there's the baby."

Aaron and Josie both reached to cover the spot where their child was growing, their fingers entwined. "I saw the doctor this week."

"What did he say?" Marla had been wondering when her mother would get around to having the pregnancy confirmed. She was also curious as to what Dr. Reynolds had to say about Josie's ability to carry a baby.

Josie chuckled at the memory. "He was surprised, to say the least, but since you had already called him four times, he was a little more prepared. He wants to run some tests on me to determine if everything is fine. An amniocentesis."

Marla wondered if Aaron was aware of the tension haunting Josie's eyes. She studied him while he assured her mother everything would be perfect. There was no denying he loved her mother, but from what Eric said she wondered if Aaron was really capable of taking on the responsibilities of husband and father.

Eric had recounted endless stories of Aaron's irresponsibility. It seemed as if Aaron lived in his own little world not subject to the regulations and demands of normal people. His art had been his life since childhood.

Marla worried he wouldn't be able to set aside a portion of himself for her mother. And their child. "Is that dangerous?"

Josie lifted her eyes and reached for Marla's hand. "The procedure is fairly routine for a woman my age. It's mainly to determine the health of the baby."

"I'm sure everything is . . ." She stumbled over her words as she caught sight of Eric watching them from the doorway. "Fine."

Eric watched Marla become aware of him. Her eyes opened in surprise, and he noticed a flare of something else before she dropped the mask she was so clever at wearing. Had that flicker been desire or was that merely wishful thinking on his part?

He spent the better part of the week thinking of her when he should have been dealing with injured skiers, cranky lifts, and lost children. Sitting in front of the stone hearth with only the dying fire for light, she was even more beautiful then he remembered. The soft glow of the flames painted a subtle halo on her hair and her eyes held the serenity of a Renaissance Madonna. He could even envision her parting the fold of her gold blouse for a child to suckle at her breast. Dang, where was that jaded character when he really needed it?

Probably the same place where it had been all week. He had become obsessed with pigeonholing her along with all the other women he knew. He had learned early in life that women were only interested in what he could do for them sexually or financially. He was ashamed to admit he played a cruel game with her trying to determine exactly what it was she expected from him. He played by his own rules and she beat him hands down.

Few women could resist the lure of the almighty dollar, and Eric suspected Marla would be as susceptible as any other woman. A dozen long-stemmed red roses—she thanked him politely. A glorious meal in the most exclusive restaurant in town—she thanked him politely and asked for a doggy bag. A small yet tasteful diamond necklace—she thanked him politely, handed back the velvet box and suggested he put his money into mutual funds.

She had been right to turn down the necklace, but it still angered him that she hadn't fallen into his trap and they ended the evening in yet another argument. This one concerning his financial investments. Marla, always the conservative with other people's money, opted for blue chip stocks and mutual funds. Eric, having more money to play with, liked over-the-counter stocks and limited partnerships. He tried for the last word by claiming that options were the quickest way to make lots of money. Marla calmly countered that options were also the quickest way to lose lots of money.

The humor of the situation hit him about halfway up the mountain after dropping Marla at her apartment. He wanted to find out her opinion of his wealth. She gave it to him all right, and if he wasn't careful, she would be charging him for services rendered.

The next evening he set out to impress her with his knowledge. Having been taught that an education was the best defense against prejudice, he worked hard in school and was darn proud of his MBA and the fact that he could answer most of the questions on *Jeopardy*.

So after dinner he slowly eased into his cerebral mode. A casual reference to Tolstoy—she asked if he knew that his principle of nonresistance to evil influenced the doctrine of passive resistance preached by Gandhi. This led to an in-depth and heated discussion of the Indian wars of the late 1800's. Eric won the battle, but he had a sneaking suspicion he was losing the war.

Last night he tried the sensual approach. It was one that never failed him. Since he had convinced Rebecca Hawthorn to go parking with him at sixteen, women had always been more than eager to share themselves with him physically. The novelty had worn off by the time he was a sophomore in college and now he was very discriminating when it came to sharing his bed.

She had been stunning in a classy purple silk pantsuit that would have looked like pajamas on anyone else. He felt a stab of jealousy as more than one man turned to watch her glide across the room.

After supper he suggested they try dancing again. Since it was Friday night, the place was packed. He took her in his arms and, because of the crowd, held her close. He did enough bumping and grinding to make Gypsy Rose Lee proud. It was working, too, he had seen it in her eyes, hot pools of need. Need that matched his own, and this time he hadn't pulled away.

After dancing he suggested they walk the three blocks to her apartment. Long, leisurely strolls were designed to put women at ease and prepare them for the kill. It also helped extremely aroused men garner some sort of control over themselves.

When they arrived at her door he was courteous, almost humble in his good-bye. She offered her lips for the good-bye kiss that had become their ritual. thinking to press his advantage, he sought to deepen the kiss— she slipped out of his arms and through the door to leave him standing on her front porch as randy as he had been with Rebecca Hawthorn.

"Good evening." He strolled up to stand by Marla's side, his hand gently clasping her shoulder.

"Hello, Eric." Marla sensed the immediate tension in the room and searched for some way to thwart the inevitable confrontation.

"Well, if it isn't Simon Legree," Aaron quipped, his lips set into thin lines.

"Aaron." Josie placed her hand on Aaron's thigh and glanced at Marla for help.

Shrugging her shoulders, Marla admitted defeat. "Isn't there someplace we can go talk? I think we could use a little privacy."

Eric and Aaron continued to stare at each other, and Marla had the impression they were about to count off ten paces and fire. "*Eric, could I speak to you, please?*"

Without breaking eye contact, he placed his hand under her arm and helped her to her feet. "Excuse us, we'll be right back."

"I look forward to it," Aaron challenged, wrapping his arm around Josie, who promptly jabbed her elbow in his ribs. "Ow, what was that for?"

Marla couldn't hear her mother's reply, but she had a good idea that Aaron would be getting the same lecture she was about to bestow on Eric. Allowing him to lead her past the bar to the storage room, Marla grinned an apology to the bartender.

"What's this all about?" Eric rounded on her the minute the door swung shut.

"I just thought you could use a little time to cool down before throwing down the gauntlet," she reasoned. She had learned that Eric's flash temper was usually just that—a flash. "You cannot go in there and start ordering him around like he was ten."

"Why not? That is how he is acting." Eric flung his

hand in the general direction of the lounge managing to knock a bottle of whiskey off a shelf.

"Eric!" Aaron threw open the door just in time to catch the bottle as it hit him in the chest. "What the heck are you doing?"

Aaron and Josie wedged themselves into the tiny room and shut the door behind them. "Marla, what's going on?"

"I was trying to calm Eric down before things escalated into a barroom brawl." Marla struggled to keep her voice down.

"I don't need anyone to calm me down," Eric shouted. "I am fine."

"There isn't any need to yell at her," Josie said, coming to her daughter's rescue. "You are acting like a raving lunatic."

"Of course I am." Eric's voice echoed around the small room, his frustration evident in the hard line of his jaw. "You people are driving me crazy. If you would only listen to reason."

"Hah," Josie countered. Aaron settled in behind her, his arms crossed over his chest. "And just whose reason would that be? *Yours?*"

"Yes, mine." In his anger, he actually shook his finger in Josie's face. "You two are acting like a couple of teenagers."

"If you want to keep that finger, get it out of my face." Josie snapped her teeth at the offending digit. "I hate to burst your dictatorial bubble here, but neither Aaron nor I are underage."

"Then why don't you act like it?" Eric shoved his hands into his pockets. "You have to see that this marriage is doomed." He lifted his eyes to Aaron. "Do you realize that when you are sixty, she'll be seventy-four?"

"Really?" Aaron's voice could have curdled milk. "Gosh, I guess I should have worked it out on the calculator. That changes everything."

"There's no need for sarcasm."

"You're right, there isn't," Aaron growled. "As a matter of fact, there isn't any need for this conversation."

"Whoa, sorry." The red-faced bartender opened the heavy wooden door. "I need a couple of things. Won't take a minute."

"Don't worry about it, Jeff." Aaron placed his hand on the small of Josie's back and led her out of the room. "The family conference is over."

"Now, wait a minute." Eric reached for Aaron's arm, but Marla quickly pulled him back as Jeff scurried to make his exit.

"Eric." she whispered. "Let them go."

"But . . ." He glanced down at her and shook his head. "They didn't listen to one thing that I said."

"And just what was it that they were supposed to listen to?" Marla asked quietly. "That they were acting like a couple of kids? For Pete's sake, my mother is older than you are."

"Then why doesn't she act like it?" Eric settled his tall frame on a large keg of beer.

"I thought we were going to tread lightly," Marla sighed, reaching over to slide her fingertips along the top of his bowed head.

"Dang." He mumbled into his hands. "You're right. I botched it up good."

Squatting down next to him, she ran her hand down his back, trying to ease the tension her fingers found there. "Don't worry about it. Give them some time to cool down and we'll try again."

Raising his head, he grinned at the closed door. "Boy, your mom's got quite a temper on her."

"Yeah, just like someone else I know." The tenor of her voice left no doubt that she was speaking of him.

"How about a bite to eat?" He held out his hand and helped her to her feet.

A loud rumbling from her stomach answered his question. She had spent the morning and half the afternoon at the office catching up on paperwork. By the time she left the office she had been in such a hurry to get up the mountain that she hadn't stopped to eat. In fact she had all but given up eating on the days when she was seeing Eric in the evening.

A grin subdued the harsh lines of his face and he caressed the small of her back as he pushed against the door. "I would say that was a yes."

"I never got around to eating today," she admitted. He gave a gentle shake of his head and pushed harder. "What's wrong?"

A small chuckle rumbled through his massive chest. "Serves me right. We're locked in."

"What?" Marla squeaked, placing her hands on the cool metal lining of the door.

"This is a storage room," Eric pointed out. "We normally don't store people in it."

"Can't Jeff let us out?"

"Oh, he'll be back eventually," Eric pointed out slowly. He was beginning to enjoy the idea of being locked up with Marla for a few hours.

"This is ridiculous." Marla beat both of her fists against the door. "Jeff!"

"Marla, he can't hear you." Eric grabbed her wrists and turned her in his arms. "This room is soundproof because of the insulation. Besides, the bar is on the other side of the room."

"But we can't just sit here," Marla argued. "We'll run out of air."

"No, we won't." Eric pointed to the cool-air fan. "We might freeze to death, but we won't suffocate."

"I don't believe this." Marla slumped against him, seeking his warmth.

"Might as well accept it." Eric slid his hands over her arms. "It could be hours before Jeff needs more supplies."

Marla tilted her head up and found her mouth inches from his. She had been concentrating so hard on their situation, she had forgotten how close he was standing. She gave a brief thought to dying in his arms before his lips descended on hers.

His almost uncontrollable desire for this beautiful, practical woman had built to a fever pitch during the last week and he reveled in finally having her in his arms. She molded herself against him, her hands sliding up to clasp around his neck. His arm slid around her slender waist pulling her tightly to him while his other hand held her head as his tongue plundered her mouth. Her thighs automatically parted to make room for him as he pressed her against the door.

Heat flared through him as her hands caressed him through his sweater. She made small, whimpering noises as his lips trailed down the silken column of her throat.

She gave a brief thought to stopping him, but then he teased the curve of her ear with his lips, his hot breath sending a series of shivers along her spine. Her fingers wound themselves in his hair as his lips continued their quest down the open neck of her blouse. One arm still held her close and his free hand slid under the deep fold of material to cup the fullness of her breast through the thin lace of her bra.

He teased the hardened tip with the pad of his thumb, causing her to cry out and buck against him. His tongue traced the edge of the delicate lace until his fingers managed to find the front closure and release her. He had dreamed of this all week, her flesh on his lips. Every night when he left her, he imagined her under him, seeking the fulfillment he could give her.

He had suspected there was a passionate woman under all her practical words and logical feelings. No one could argue the way she did without passion. In that respect they had a great deal in common. Her passion fueled his own and he felt his arousal pressing painfully against his zipper.

He pulled her fully against him and she felt the hem of her skirt riding up on her thighs as he pressed his knee between her legs. He cupped her bottom to raise her higher against the door. She felt his fingers on the chilly flesh of her thigh and heard him growl as he realized that instead of panty hose she wore a garter belt and stockings.

"What about Jeff?" She pushed against his chest, determined to regain her composure.

"Let him find his own girl," Eric murmured into her neck.

"Eric, stop." Pushing his hands away from her, Marla hurriedly tidied her clothing. "I don't like this."

He raised one eyebrow at her words. "Lady, you like this as much as I do."

"All right," she whispered. "I can't deny that. But," she held up her hand to stop him from taking her back in his arms, "I don't think this is the proper place to further our relationship."

Eric ran his hand over his face and grimaced at their surroundings. "Marla, I have never been one to lock my women in closets and jump them. I guess I got a little carried away."

"I guess we both did." She placed her hand on his arm, needing to maintain some kind of contact with him. He immediately pulled her into his embrace and they clung together.

"Hey, boss." Jeff burst into the room, ending the need for further conversation. "I just realized you might be locked in here."

Shielding Marla from Jeff's curious eyes, Eric thanked the young man and rushed them out of the room and through the lounge. "Let's go up to my apartment."

"I need to stop in here." She hurried into the ladies' room before he could stop her. Forcing herself to look in the mirror, she cringed. Her hair stuck out in all directions and she didn't have any makeup left. Her lips were swollen and her hands shook. All of that would have been fine if it weren't for the hunger still lingering in her eyes. She looked like a woman who had just enjoyed an appetizer and was ready for the main course.

She twisted the gold knob on the faucet and plunged her hands under the ice cold water. She had to get hold of herself before she faced Eric again.

Some small part of her had been waiting for this. The first time his lips touched hers he had started a small flame of desire deep inside her and had fed the fire by keeping her constantly aware of herself as a woman. A fleeting touch was enough to send shivers down her spine. A smoldering glance sent all rational thought from her head. For the first time in her life she understood why her mother had wound up pregnant. When Eric touched her she could deny him nothing.

He could have had her naked in seconds if he had wanted, despite the fact they were in a storage room.

She covered her mouth to muffle the sob threatening to escape. How had he managed to do the one thing she would have sworn was impossible? How had he managed to sneak past her carefully constructed defenses and touch her where no one had ever touched her before?

Her mother was right, love did just pop up and hit you over the head. She hadn't even seen it coming.

SIX

"Thanks, Jeff." Eric lifted the shot glass and downed it. The liquid burned a trail down his throat and tears sprang to his eyes. Served him right.

He quickly filled the glass with water and sought to quench the fire in his belly. Except it wasn't a flame to be doused with water. What had possessed him to act like some sex-starved teenager? Marla.

He uttered an earthy phrase, one his grandmother would have washed his mouth out with soap for, and stalked across the lounge. He glanced at his watch. It had been more than twenty minutes since Marla had escaped to the privacy of the rest room. What could be taking her so long? She was probably plotting his murder. And he couldn't blame her.

He wouldn't bother to lie to himself about what just transpired. They were too combustible together for it not to have happened. But he hadn't meant to go so fast, and certainly not in a storeroom.

His eyes finally came to rest on the coat rack where her heavy wool coat had hung earlier. It was gone and so was Marla.

Eric sank down onto the nearest couch and buried his head in his hands. How had things gotten so out of hand?

The longer Eric thought about what had passed between them and Marla's stealthy departure the more furious he became. She didn't have any right to treat him like this. No right at all. If she was upset, fine. All she had to do was talk to him about it. At least he would have had a chance to defend his actions . . . or apologize.

It only took a second for him to grab his jacket and make his way out the front door. If she thought she could get away from him this easily, she had another think coming.

Marla's heels clicked on the concrete as she hurried up the steps to her apartment. Adjusting her grip on the bag containing her dinner, she felt around in the bottom of her purse for her keys. Why had she put them in her purse? Just one more thing designed to ruin her evening.

"Where the hell have you been?" Eric snarled as she reached the top of the stairs leading to her apartment.

"Eric!" She jerked back as he stepped toward her and would have fallen down the steep flight of stairs had he not grabbed her arm. "What are you doing here?"

"Open the door," he ordered. "I don't really want to have this conversation on your front porch."

For a split second she thought about refusing, but she didn't have any desire to air her dirty laundry in front of her bevy of nosy neighbors, either.

"Give me those," he commanded after her third attempt. He quickly unlocked the door and slipped inside to flip on the lights.

Marla hurriedly passed him before he got really macho and decided to sling her over his shoulder and carry her in the house. "You don't have any rights . . ."

"Rights!" He bellowed as soon as he had closed the door, flinging his arms in all directions. "You want to talk about rights? Fine. What gave you the right to disappear on me tonight? I've been out of my mind."

Marla refused to join in a shouting match with him. "I'm sorry if you were worried, but you didn't have to come down the mountain. You could have called."

"What good would that have done me, you weren't home," he pointed out at the top of his lungs.

"I needed some time to myself," she reasoned. "To think."

Eric shoved his fingers though his hair with a cry of frustration. "That doesn't explain why you had to sneak out." Eric's anger fizzled into a useless emotion. "I thought we shared something pretty special."

Marla turned away from the confusion in his eyes. How could she explain what she didn't understand herself? "It shouldn't have happened."

Eric came up behind her and hauled her back against him. She could feel his muscles ripple and bunch as he wrapped his arms around her. "Marla, nothing really happened. I admit it's a little sudden, but what's wrong with it?"

"We're only feeling these things because of the situations we keep finding ourselves in. They aren't real," she argued, not liking the desperation tinting her voice or the way she felt in his arms.

Eric turned her to face him. Needing to see the truth in her eyes as much as he wanted her to find it in his own. "This is real, Marla. I don't know what it is, but I do know that it isn't due to circumstances, or situations.''

There were so many things she wanted to say, questions she needed to ask, but once his lips found hers they flew from her mind. Only hours ago she had no idea of where this mindless pleasure would lead, but now her body throbbed with a new awareness as his tongue probed into the heated recess of her mouth.

Desire coiled deep inside her waiting for the release that would send her soaring. Her body arched of its own accord until her aching breasts were pressed against him. She briefly thought of making some token protest before dragging him down the hall to the bedroom, but her words were muffled by his lips and once more she gave in to the wonder of his kiss.

"This is how is should be." He lifted her effortlessly in his arms and carried her down the hallway to her bedroom. In the darkness of the room he fell across the bed with her still in his arms. His hands trembled slightly as he tugged the hem of her blouse free from her skirt. "I'm not made for quickies in the closet, either. I want to love you, Marla, every beautiful square inch."

She marveled he was at least partially affected by the situation. He laid her against the pillows and she watched in fascination as he quickly divested himself of his jeans and shirt.

Even in the darkness of the bedroom she could see the magnificence of his body. Her eyes traced the muscled contours of his chest, down the flat plane of his stomach until they reached the part of him designed to fit inside her.

She quickly averted her eyes from the evidence of his desire as he came to lay beside her on the bed. The fear forgotten only moments before now reared its ugly head and she clenched her eyes tightly shut.

"I'll take care of you."

Misunderstanding him, Marla grabbed his hand. She assumed he intended to "take care of her" as he had before. If she was going to do this, it would be as an equal partner. "It's okay."

Eric had been reaching for his wallet and the small foil packet he had placed there a few days ago. Her shyness had caused him to question her experience, but her words helped to assure him she knew what she was doing.

Eric lowered himself down next to her so that she was pressed against the length of him. He could feel the small trembles quaking through her and slid his arm under her neck to hold her to him. She snuggled against him and let his hands soothe away her fears. He felt a protective urge that unbalanced him.

Her apprehension was clear and he could only assume her past lovers had not taken the time to ensure her satisfaction. He knew a lot of men were like that, only concerned with seeking their own fulfillment. Damn fools. They had no idea of what lovemaking was all about.

Apparently, due to some guy's insensitivity, neither did Marla. "We'll take it as slow as you want, honey. I'm in no hurry."

His fingers became slightly more aggressive, drawing gasps and sighs from her as they flicked over her sensitized skin. Under his touch even her elbows became erogenous zones. Pressing herself against him, she readily opened for his touch.

He prayed she was ready for him because his control was slipping like sand through his fingers. He had never derived such pleasure from a woman's touch, especially when she hadn't even ventured below his navel.

He shifted her under him and parted her legs. Her eyes fluttered shut and he placed a delicate kiss on each lid before taking her mouth with his. He used his tongue to show her the rhythm they would share. "Are you ready for me?"

"I . . ." Ready for him? She was ready to explode! "I . . ." She could feel his fingers probing into the moist heat of her flesh, testing her, opening her for him.

The ringing of the phone blurted into the silence of the room startling them both.

"Damn!" Eric growled. Why hadn't they remembered to take the phone off the hook? "Let it ring."

Marla struggled out from under him. "I can't. It might be Mom. Something could be wrong."

Eric flung himself back on the pillows and threw his arm over his eyes. His body was taut and aching from the restraint he had shown over the past few minutes.

Marla managed to grab the receiver before knocking the phone onto the floor. Her breath was harsh and there was a decided whine in her voice. "Hello?"

"Marla, this is Aaron."

"Aaron!" Marla sat up in bed, disregarding the sheet that now fell to her waist. "What's wrong?"

Eric had also sat up after hearing his brother's name. "Does he want me?"

"Marla, is that Eric?" Aaron seemed surprised to hear his brother's voice, and Marla could hear him relaying the information to her mother. "Well, that just saves me a call. We wanted to let you know that we are on our way to Las Vegas."

"Las Vegas!" Marla repeated, and Eric jerked the receiver from her hand.

"Aaron, what are you talking about?" he demanded, turning his pent-up frustration on his brother. "Where are you?"

"What are you doing at Marla's?" Aaron relayed the question from Josie.

"None of your business," Eric growled, and slid his legs off the side of the bed to search for his pants. "You can't be serious about Las Vegas."

"Let me talk to Marla," Aaron demanded, refusing to answer his brother.

Eric recognized the petulant tone of Aaron's voice and knew it would do no good to reason with him. "Here."

Marla debated switching on the light. Part of her wanted to remain in darkness, safe from Eric's eyes. The other part, the logical part, told her not to be ridiculous. She had been about to share her body with the man in the most intimate way possible, what difference could it make if he saw her naked. "Aaron, may I speak to Mother?"

Eric took a moment for his eyes to adjust to the light. His clothes were scattered from one end of the room to the other. He would have to strut buck-naked across the room just to get his underwear. How had this happened to a man who folded his socks before putting them in the dirty clothes hamper?

He could hear Marla trying to reason with her mother, but from the sound of things she wasn't making any more progress than he had with Aaron. She turned her back to him and he took the opportunity to grab her robe from the rocking chair next to his side of the bed. It was too short and too tight, but at least it wasn't pink and frilly.

"Mother, please," Marla begged. "Mother?"

"What's wrong?" he asked, stooping to pick up one black sock.

Marla felt lightheaded as she watched the hem of her robe ride up, revealing more than half of his masculine backside. If they had turned the lights on earlier she would have jerked the phone out of the wall before interrupting their lovemaking. Eric Westbrook was gorgeous!

Eric felt the cool air on his backside and hurriedly straightened. So far he had only managed to locate his underwear, pants, and one sock. "Have you seen my shirt?"

Marla forced her eyes from his legs and scanned the room. "It's over there."

Eric strode to the corner and plucked his shirt off the curtain rod where it hung like a red flag. "What did Aaron have to say?"

Marla tugged the sheet loose from the mattress and wrapped it mummy-style around her. "Just that they were driving to Vegas to be married. He wouldn't tell me what town they were in or where they would be staying once he found out you were here."

"You sound like it's my fault." He slipped behind her bathroom door and quickly slid into his clothes. Tonight sure wasn't ending the way he had planned it.

"It *is* your fault," Marla reasoned. She grabbed a pair of underpants from her dresser drawer and hurriedly slipped them over her hips. "If you weren't so insistent on having everything your way, they wouldn't be doing this."

"I do not insist on having everything my way," he argued.

"Yes, you do." She stepped into a pair of navy linen pants and searched through her closet for the navy-and-green sweater she usually wore with them. "You made them do this."

Eric was shocked at her irrationality. Every time they argued in the past, he had admired her sense of reason. She always had facts and figures to back up her opinion. Now she was acting like a . . . well, like a woman.

He stepped from the bathroom just in time to catch a glimpse of her naked breasts before the colorful knit sweater covered them. "Marla, you are being ridiculous. You agreed with me that this marriage was a mistake."

She poked her head through the neck of the sweater and found herself staring into his eyes. Even through his anger she recognized his lust. A small curl of desire settled low in her belly and she quickly turned from him. "I have changed my mind."

"Isn't that just like a woman," he quipped, and ducked as her hairbrush whizzed past his head. "What do you think you're doing."

"Trying to bash you upside the head." Although she never raised her voice, she was shocked at her actions. She had never thrown anything in her life. Not even a softball.

But she guessed that was to be expected. Since meeting Eric she hardly recognized herself. Several times during the week she caught herself staring up at the mountain, wondering. What was he doing? Who was he doing it with? Hundreds of nagging little thoughts that crept into her daily rituals, driving her insane with their tenacity.

"I could have figured that part out by myself." He smirked, picking the brush up off the floor and running it over the thick mass of his black hair. "I meant, where do you think you're going?"

Marla slid a pair of soft navy leather boots out of their designated place in the back of her closet and tugged them on over her half-hose. "You're going after them, aren't you?"

"Yes," he answered, tucking his shirt into his pants and zipping them.

She grabbed her overnight bag from its hook on the inside of the closet door and hurriedly filled it with a few items of clothing. She pushed past Eric and grabbed her makeup bag and toothbrush off the vanity. "I'm going with you."

"No." The word was heartfelt.

"Fine." Now was not the time to waste on an unnecessary argument. "Maybe I'll run into you."

"I said you weren't going with me." He tugged on the strap of her bag, pulling her back until she was next to him.

"Listen . . ." She jabbed a fingernail into the center of his chest, "I'm going after my mother. You're not my father, my husband, my boyfriend, or my lover. You don't have anything to say about the matter."

Eric opened his mouth and quickly closed it. Why was he arguing? If he were totally honest with himself, he had to admit he wanted her to come with him. "I'm sorry."

Marla flicked off the bedroom light, leaving them in darkness. "You're what?"

"Don't push it," he grumbled, but she heard the teasing lilt under his words.

Marla took his hand and led him down the short hallway to the living room She switched on the small Tiffany lamp she always lighted when she was gone.

"I plan to fly," he felt honor-bound to warn her.

Dang! She should have known he would fly up to Las Vegas. After the stink she had just put up there was no way she could back out now without looking like an idiot. "No problem." She only hoped he had a good supply of air-sickness bags.

SEVEN

Eric expertly maneuvered the plane into position and within minutes they were airborne. "You can open your eyes now."

"Very funny." How had he known her eyes were shut?

The stars winked at them in the velvet blanket of the night. Somehow not being able to see the ground so far below them was less frightening than actual visible proof of their altitude. Marla felt her fingers loosen their death grip on the armrest.

"It will only take a couple of hours," he assured. "You okay?"

"I'm fine." She heard his snort of disbelief. "Why wouldn't I be? There is nothing to be afraid of." She said the chanted words like a mantra.

"There's nothing wrong with a little fear." He tried to ease her discomfort.

Marla sat up higher in her seat, her chin tilting up just a fraction. "I am not afraid."

Eric chuckled, recognizing her "fighter" stance even in the dim light of the instrument panel. "I believe you."

"You do not," she grumbled, and turned to stare out into the darkness. "I'm not afraid of anything."

"Oh, really." His voice had dropped to a husky whisper and she knew he was recalling how she had trembled earlier when he had carried her to the bedroom.

"Yes, really," she quipped. "I have a healthy respect for rattlesnakes and I don't especially like spiders, but I'm not afraid of them."

"What about me?" he teased.

"What *about* you?" She feigned ignorance.

"You're afraid of me," he whispered. "You're afraid of what I make you feel."

"Don't flatter yourself." She strived for just the right amount of derision.

"It's okay, you know. I'm afraid of it, too," he found himself admitting. What was wrong with him? This had gone beyond small talk to keep her mind off the flight, this was dangerously close to "true confessions."

When Marla didn't answer him, Eric decided it would be more expedient to let the matter drop. He knew it had been more than desire that had caused her to tremble in his arms.

Oh, the desire had been there, of that he had no doubt. But underneath there had been just the slightest bit of apprehension and, whether she wanted to admit it or not, fear. The same fear he had experienced when her small sighs and moans had crept their way into his heart and touched him in a way that no woman had ever done.

The flight to Las Vegas took only the few hours Eric had promised and it was still dark when Marla noticed the myriad of lights winking at them in the distance. The small cluster of flickering lights quickly grew into a mass of neon that could be easily seen from the air.

"Have you ever seen so many lights?" she marveled as their course took them over the heart of the city.

"A few times." He watched her face light up as bright as the city below them and he felt an uneasy feeling in the pit of his stomach. He wanted to be the one who put that look on her face. He wanted her to look at him like he was the Las Vegas strip and she was a compulsive gambler with a fistful of money. He wanted *her*.

Marla realized he had probably been there several times and how childish she must sound to him. Trying to make up for her momentary lapse of poise, she settled back in the seat refusing to take another glance at the wonderful sight below her. "How are we going to go about finding them in all that?"

Eric noticed she had replaced her mask of indifference and frowned. Why wouldn't she let him see her true feelings? Was she so afraid of them herself that she couldn't allow anyone else to know they existed? It was a sad thought and one he wasn't up to contemplating right now. "I called a friend of mine here in Vegas earlier, so things should already be started."

"A friend?" When had he made the call? "What things?"

"Yeah, Geri should already have someone calling the chapels to see if Aaron made a reservation." He broke off to converse with the air traffic controller at the small airfield in front of them.

"What is that?" Marla released the armrest long enough to point to the narrow strip of asphalt illuminated by twin rows of lights.

"The runway," he answered, and tipped the front of the plane down.

"Oh my Lord," Marla whispered, throwing her hands over her eyes. What was she doing? She didn't want to die on some dirty stretch of ground in Nevada.

"Relax, sweetheart." He longed to pull her into his arms and soothe her, but the landing required all of his attention.

Her ears began to pop due to their descent and she thought briefly of the stick of gum she had swallowed during takeoff. She uncovered her eyes and swore she would face death just as she had always faced life; with both eyes open. The ground rushed by at an alarming rate and she wondered why Eric didn't put on the brakes.

"Here we go." She watched his hands as he lowered the plane the last few feet. Marla felt a slight bump and then they were jiggling down the runway, leaving her heart permanently lodged in her throat.

"You can let go now, babe." Eric patted her hand before prying her fingers from the armrest. He slid out his side of the plane and hurried around to hers. When she had told him she was not a good flier, he hadn't expected outright terror. "Do you want to kiss the ground or anything?"

Ignoring him, Marla hurried toward the small cluster of buildings just off the runway. "Are we meeting this friend of yours?" she asked as they made their way through the almost deserted airport terminal.

"Sure." Eric glanced at the doorway and an enormous grin lit up his face. "Right about now."

Marla watched in horror as Eric left her side to grab a tall redhead around the waist and lift her off the ground. The gorgeous woman planted a loud kiss on his lips and Marla gave careful consideration to yanking every shiny red hair that hung down the woman's back. "Excuse me."

Eric heard the ice in Marla's voice and it warmed him all the way down to his toes. He had purposely kept Geri's gender a secret just to see if it would get a rise out of Marla. If the tilt of her chin was any indication, he had been more than successful. "Marla Crandall, I'd like you to meet Geri Halifax, the best P.I. in town."

"P.I.?" Marla hoped she didn't look as stunned as she felt. This woman was a private investigator? Marla took in the over-size flannel shirt, the slouchy blue jeans, and scuffed black army boots of the woman in front of her. She glanced back up at the exotically tilted green eyes, patrician nose, and full lips and tried to equate them with the rest of the picture. Why on earth was a woman who looked like Geri Halifax dressed like a derelict?

"I'm glad to meet you, Marla." Geri wiggled out of Eric's arms and held out her hand. "Don't mind Pook here, he only does that because he knows I hate it."

"Pook?" Marla didn't even try not to grin, noticing the pained expression that sprang to Eric's face.

"Geri!" Eric growled, and took a menacing step toward his friend.

"Now, Pook," Geri warned, planting her feet. "You know what happened last time you took that tone with me."

Eric remembered and stopped his advance. "You wouldn't dare."

"The hell I wouldn't," Geri promised and grinned at Marla's confusion. "The last time this brute threatened me, he wound up flat on his back. I wasn't a Marine for nothing, you know."

Marla's confusion went from bad to worse. "You were in the Marines?"

"Sure, that's where I met Eric, didn't he tell you."

Geri asked, and then proceeded to answer her own question. "No, of course, he didn't tell you. He was probably hoping to stir up a little jealousy and see how far it would get him. Well, don't worry."

"I'm not worried. I couldn't care less." Marla tilted her chin up and headed for the ladies' room and a few minutes of peace to compose herself.

"Pook, why can't you leave well enough alone?" Geri turned on Eric the second Marla disappeared behind the door. "You sure got her dander up coming at me like that. She's madder than a wet hen."

"I intended to 'get her dander up,' as you so charmingly put it." Eric's grin turned to a grimace. "And quit calling me Pook."

"I'll try, but I'm afraid you'll always be Pook to me." Geri slapped him on his jean-clad rear end and headed for the ladies' room.

Marla had just finished freshening her lipstick when Geri burst through the door. "Honey, don't worry about it. You have got that man out there so confused he doesn't know if he's coming or going."

"Eric? Confused?" Marla sniffed. "I think we must be talking about two different men."

Geri settled one hip on the counter and pulled a pack of cigarettes out of her shirt pocket. "You could be right about that."

Marla watched Geri light her cigarette and inhale deeply. The image didn't fit. Geri Halifax had to be the most beautiful woman Marla had ever seen, yet she talked, acted, and dressed like she was straight off an oil rig in West Texas. She watched the woman take another drag on her cigarette before laying it on the side of the sink to burrow her long fingers into that mass of hair and quickly plait it into a single braid down her back.

"Why do you say that?"

" 'Cause Eric is pretty good at letting people see only what he wants them to." Geri shrugged and dug into her jean pocket for a rubber band to fasten the end of her braid. She picked up the almost forgotten cigarette and flipped her ashes into the sink. "Aaron gets Papa Eric, I get Pook, and you get Loverboy."

"But we aren't lovers," Marla protested, and felt her cheeks burn under the half-truth. Why couldn't she learn to control these blushes? They gave her away every time.

"Maybe not now, but you will be." Geri took one last drag and flicked the butt into one of the toilets. "I don't think either one of you has any say so about that."

Marla started to argue but held her tongue. It wouldn't do any good. Geri had seen what Marla had been struggling to keep hidden from everyone else. Was her love for Eric so obvious? Had he seen it?

"Don't worry, kid," Geri assured her with an easy confidence as they made their way back to Eric. "He doesn't even know he's in love with you yet."

Marla couldn't see what the big deal was. In the new light of day Las Vegas looked like a perfectly normal city instead of the teeming den of iniquity she had expected.

So far, the most exciting part of the trip was Geri's driving. Wedged between Geri and Eric in the cab of the glossy black pickup, Marla found herself clinging to Eric as they flew around every corner in downtown Las Vegas.

She cast a desperate glance at Eric, who only shook his head and grinned as Geri took another corner on what felt like two wheels.

"Here we are," Geri cut the wheel sharply to the

right and slid into a tiny parking spot more suited to a golf cart than the enormous three-quarter-ton pickup. She patted Marla on the knee. "Come on, let's go see what Boris found out."

"Boris?" Eric and Marla questioned the air where Geri had been.

Eric helped her out of the pickup and they followed Geri into the dingy storefront that housed the Halifax and Son Private Investigation Agency. "Halifax and Son?"

"Geri's dad wanted a boy," Eric explained as he held the door open for Marla. "He had the sign painted the day he found out his wife was pregnant and just never changed it."

Marla and Eric strode to the back of the building where Geri was in deep conversation with a large, bald man. "Did you tell Sarah to call if anything showed up?"

In lieu of reply the large man's eyebrows rose to an arch over his brilliant blue eyes and he crossed his massive arms over his chest. Geri got the message. "Sorry, Boris. I have complete confidence in your abilities."

Eric and Marla stood a few feet away from the odd couple, loath to interrupt. Finally, Eric couldn't stand not knowing. "Geri, have you found anything?"

Geri jerked her head up from the form she had been perusing and her eyes widened as if she had forgotten their presence. "Sorry, Pook. You know me and my one-track mind." She rummaged in her desk drawer. "Boris, have you been hiding my cigarettes again?"

"It does no good," the big man bemoaned in a surprisingly gentle voice. Marla could detect the lingering traces of a Russian accent and her curiosity was fired.

"Geri, they're in your shirt pocket," Marla offered.

This was the woman who was supposed to help find her mother?

"Thanks," Geri mumbled around the filtered tip as she grabbed a matchbook off the overflowing pile on her desk. She handed Eric the sheet of paper she had been studying. "This is the list of all couples who have filed for a marriage license within the last forty-eight hours."

Eric quickly scanned the neatly typed list. "They aren't on it."

"No sh—shoot, Sherlock." Geri shot Marla an apologetic grin. "But that list is only up to midnight last night, they could be at the license bureau right now."

"Shouldn't we stake the place out?" Eric asked, heading for the door.

"Hold up there, Speedy." Geri plopped down in her chair. "That's what you're paying me for, remember? I've got a man stationed at the bureau. Boris will also check with a friendly clerk every thirty minutes."

"Then what are we supposed to do in the meantime?" Eric hated letting someone else take over the reins. He had been running the show for so long that it was almost impossible for him to let Geri do her job even though he knew she was better prepared to find his brother than he was. She had the contacts that would make things progress much more smoothly than his bungled attempts would.

"I suggest you start hitting the wedding chapels," Geri advised. "They could have gotten their license in another town, although it's doubtful. Not every town in Nevada has a license bureau that stays open on weekends like Vegas. They would had to have gotten it on Friday."

"No, Mom and Aaron were both at the lodge yesterday evening,'' Marla said, desperate to be of some help.

"Look, kids . . ." Geri lifted her boot-clad feet onto her desk and leaned back in her chair. "I'm betting that they left last night for Vegas. They either stopped along the way or drove straight through. I figure they'll head for the bureau sometime late this morning and to a chapel right after."

"Then how are we going to stop them?" Eric asked.

"I've been meaning to ask you about that, Pook." Geri dug another cigarette out of her pocket and lit it before continuing. "I normally don't ask why, but I am now."

"Geri, you know Aaron," Eric pointed out, helping himself to a large glass of water. "He's like a big kid. No responsibility for anything. Now he's gotten himself mixed up with this woman . . ."

"That woman happens to be my mother." Marla interrupted. "I don't appreciate the way you make her sound like some dime-store floozy."

Eric continued as if Marla hadn't even spoken. "She says she's pregnant, and Aaron wants to marry her. She's old enough to be his mother for crying out loud!"

"Ooh!" Marla understood it all now. She was fully capable of sympathizing with mass murderers. So intense was her anger at Eric that she could have gladly taken a baseball bat to his ego-inflated head. Where was the fireplace poker when she really needed it? Pushing past Eric, she stalked out the door, mindless of the fact that she had just caused him to pour water down the front of his shirt.

"Where are you going?" Eric stared after Marla for a second before turning his eyes to Geri. "Has she lost her mind?"

"Offhand I'd say she lost her temper, you big oaf."

Geri grinned at his confusion. "Pook, let me offer you a bit of advice. Never put down a woman's family and never, ever, under any circumstances, ignore her."

"I didn't," he protested, taking a towel from Boris.

"Whatever you say, Pook," Geri giggled and stood up to follow Marla.

"Quit calling me Pook!" he bellowed after her, and glanced at Boris for conformation that he hadn't lost his mind.

Boris simply raised those expressive eyebrows and handed him a shirt.

Eric slipped out of his soaking-wet pullover and flung the bright-purple T-shirt Boris had given him over his head. The hem hung halfway down his thighs and the slogan across the back proclaimed him the world's largest source of natural gas, but it was dry and would do until he could pick up something else. "Thanks, Boris."

The twinkle in those blue eyes belied the indifference etched on the large man's face as he watched Eric take after the two women at a trot. "He must learn to control his tongue."

EIGHT

Marla had gone two blocks before her anger cooled enough for her to realize she had no idea where she was going. She slowed her pace to a leisurely stroll by the time Geri caught up with her.

"That's some temper you got on you, girl." Geri jogged up next to her and offered her a cigarette.

"Do you realize that you never actually smoke those things?" Marla asked as Geri slid a match along the sandpapered edge of the matchbook and lit yet another cigarette. "You light them and take maybe two drags off them before pressing them down."

"Very observant," Geri grumbled, unused to having her quirks pointed out. "Need a job?"

"No, but I may need a good lawyer if I have to be around that man much longer." Marla could feel some of her initial anger returning just at the thought of Eric and his macho behavior. "I have the feeling I'm going to kill him before all this is over."

"I don't blame you," Geri agreed, and steered Marla down a side street. "Pook can be a handful. He's so used to being responsible for everyone around him that

90

it slops over on to anyone he meets. I've seen him order complete strangers around. The funny thing is, I've never known anyone besides me who doesn't ask 'how high' when he says 'jump'.''

Marla stopped in front of a little boutique to admire the red silk jump suit hanging in the window. "I'm used to my own responsibilities.''

"Like your mom?'' Geri tossed her cigarette to the sidewalk and stubbed it out with the toe of her army boots.

"Yeah, after my dad died she was a basket case.'' Marla watched Geri's scuffed boot twist the tobacco into the cement. "All she could do was lie in bed and cry. I finally managed to make her see that she couldn't solve anything by doing that.''

Geri stopped in front of a diner that boasted an all-you-can-eat breakfast for $1.99. "Come on, I'll buy you a cup of coffee.''

The small diner was already busy with businessmen heading to work and tourists grabbing a bite before heading to Hoover Dam. Geri and Marla chose a corner booth, and when the waitress came for their order they both ordered the special.

"I didn't realize how hungry I was until I smelled that bacon,'' Marla confessed.

"Either that or you worked up an appetite by sparring with Eric.'' Geri grinned at the memory.

Marla buried her face in her hands and moaned at the memory. "I know you won't believe it, but I never act like this. I'm famous for my cool head. The guys at my office call me the Ice Princess behind my back.''

Geri took a sip of the scalding coffee and added an ice cube to the black liquid. "Listen, Princess. Pook can get under anybody's skin with his dictatorial attitude. I've had to get physical with him a time or two myself.''

"Why do you call him Pook?" Marla realized that no one had answered her question about that earlier.

"Mainly because he hates it," Geri admitted, her green eyes sparkling with mischief. "It started when we were in the service together. There was a whole bunch of us who hung around together. We all had nicknames of some sort."

"What was yours?" Marla took her plate from the waitress and groaned at the amount of food piled on it. There was no way she could eat this much.

"Geriatric." The redhead frowned. "Not very original, I'm afraid."

"How did Eric get the nickname Pook?" She could think of a lot of things to call Eric Westbrook, but Pook wasn't one of them.

"Have you ever met Nana and Gram?" Geri asked, dumping half a bottle of ketchup on her scrambled eggs, oblivious to the disgust marring Marla's face.

"No." Josie had mentioned meeting the two grandmothers when she and Aaron took a trip to the reservation. From Josie's description they were like two matriarchal peas in a pod.

"Well, Nana has a thing about cussing," Geri explained, dunking her toast into the gooey mess on her plate. "When Eric's sister Lanie brought them out to San Diego for a visit, Eric had a hard time watching his language. It gets a little rough in the Corps."

"So I've heard." Marla stared at the clock on the wall, the baby across the aisle, the fly on the venetian blind. Anything but the goop Geri was eating.

"Anyway, Eric would say 'pook' whenever he really wanted to use a more, shall we say, earthy phrase."

"And it stuck." Marla could imagine the ribbing

Eric must have taken about it. She didn't want to like the fact that he had been willing to undergo such teasing just to keep his grandmother happy, but she did. She liked it a lot. Any man who was willing to go through that couldn't be all bad.

"I thought it was pretty nice, too," Geri admitted as if reading Marla's mind. "Of course, it was too good an opportunity to deflate that enormous psyche of his."

Marla managed to choke down a piece of dry toast as she watched Geri finish her breakfast. Geri was a mystery. With her looks she could have been a model or an actress. She acted more like a ranch hand—or like a woman trying to act like the boy her father really wanted.

With this insight tucked firmly inside her brain, Marla looked at Geri with different eyes. As many times as she had felt guilty about being the reason for her parents' marriage, she had never felt unwanted. Even Granny Crandall had been forced to admit that Marla was the only good thing to come from that mistake.

All these years she was the only one who had ever thought of herself as the mistake rather than just the fact that her parents hadn't used good judgment. Poor Geri, had she been forced to live her whole life trying to make up for not being born a male?

Just like you've spent your whole life trying to make up for the fact that you were born period, a tiny voice insisted inside her head. Was it true? Had she been so concerned with not causing her parents a minute's worth of trouble that she had forced herself into some Wonder Girl mold?

She let her mind wander back to her father's death. She could remember wanting nothing more than to crawl up in that big bed with her mother and cry. She desperately needed the reassurance that she hadn't done anything wrong. Something that had made her father die.

Instead, she watched her mother grieve until it became clear that Marla would have to take up where her father left off. She would have to be the responsible one in the family now. She would have to make the decisions that her father would have made.

And she had, she realized with a start. Here she was, pitying poor Geri because she lived her life more as a man than a woman, and she was every bit as bad. She lived her life for her father. Instead of allowing her own personality to take charge of her life, she conformed to her father's standard. Only with Eric did the true Marla break through.

It was the true Marla who loved sparring with him at the drop of a hat, and the true Marla who had longed to make love with him last night. Most of all, it was the true Marla who had fallen in love with him. Now the question was, how did she go about learning to let this Marla, her true self, live her own life? It was a scary thought, but it excited her all the same.

"Come on, we better go find Eric." Geri intruded on Marla's self-analysis. "You okay?"

"Sure." Marla nodded. "Why?"

Geri shrugged her shoulders and plucked the check up off the table. "I don't know, you looked sort of spaced out there for a minute."

"That's ridiculous," Marla muttered, unused to having her moods so easily read.

The two women hadn't gone more than a block in the direction of the office when Eric found them. "Where have you been?"

"Breakfast," Geri informed him in a tone that told him to watch his mouth if he knew what was good for him. She liked Marla and didn't want Eric to blow it before he realized how much he liked her, too. "Marla needed a few minutes to cool down."

"I'll say," Eric grumbled, and held both his hands up in surrender as the two women stopped in the middle of the sidewalk to glare at him. "No fair, two against one."

"All's fair in love and war," Geri quipped. "Which is this?"

"War!" Marla and Eric uttered simultaneously.

"Um hum." Geri grinned and climbed in the black monster she called a pickup.

"Do we have to go with you?" Marla asked, hoping the answer would be no.

"You can stay here if you want." Geri shrugged. "I'm going to the license bureau and then I'll start hitting the chapels."

"I'm coming," Eric said, and opened the passenger door. "You coming or staying?"

"Coming." Marla moaned at the thought of Geri's driving. She would have loved to stay behind with Boris, but on the off chance they did find her mother and Aaron, she wanted to be there.

Not to talk them out of the marriage, she realized with a shock, but to help them fight against Eric. Her mother and Aaron had the right to their own lives and their own mistakes. She had made too big a mess of her own life to be telling someone else how to live theirs.

The marriage-license bureau was in a small white building in the middle of downtown Las Vegas. Even though it was only ten-thirty in the morning there was already a steady stream of couples heading in and out the door.

Marriage was big business in this town with more chapels per capita than anywhere else in the world. Marla had a feeling there would be no way to track her mother and Aaron if they missed them at the license bureau.

"Do you have to bribe them to get the names?" Marla asked Geri as they crossed the street and joined the line of happy couples inside.

"Nah." Geri fished in her empty pocket for her cigarettes. "Once you apply for the license it becomes a matter of public record. You just have to know who to ask for what."

"Oh." Marla found she was a little disappointed that it was so easy. She envisioned Geri palming money to one of the clerks in the back room in order to get access to the files.

Instead, she asked for a woman named Sarah, who promptly told them that there was no record of an Aaron Westbrook or Josie Crandall. "Who are these people, Geri?"

"Nobody important." Geri grinned. "Just a little domestic case for a friend."

Marla noticed the disappointment on the other woman's face. She had probably been expecting international thieves or something. Listening to Geri explain it as a little domestic case, Marla felt embarrassed that she and Eric had spent all this time and effort on a venture that was largely based on their own vanity.

"Anything?" Eric asked when they returned to the pickup.

"Nope. You find out anything at the chapel?" Geri asked, nodding at the small wedding chapel directly across the street from the bureau.

"Nothing." Eric narrowed his eyes as he watched

another couple make their way into the bureau. "There they are!"

"Where?" Marla and Geri turned in unison to catch a glimpse of the couple before the door closed.

"Come on," Eric urged, loping across the street, narrowly missing the fender of a taxi that turned the corner in front of him.

"Eric, wait!" Marla shrieked as she watched the near-miss. Her heart was pounding so hard she thought it might burst. That idiot, he was almost killed. And for what?

That was the question. She had already come to the realization behind her actions, but she didn't think Eric had ever stopped to wonder why he was so intent on running Aaron's life.

"Was that them?" Geri asked as the two women made their way carefully across the street.

"I don't think so," Marla said. "The man looked like Aaron, but the woman was much too tall to be Mom. Mom is only five two and her hair is much blonder."

"Damn," Geri bit out. "I'll bet dollars to doughnuts Eric just charged in there like a bull. Act first, ask questions later."

The cacophony that greeted them in the bureau made any more conversation impossible. Men were shouting at each other and women were crying, glass was breaking, and there in the middle of it all was Eric laying on the floor being hit over the head with a woman's purse.

"Look what you did to my Ralph!" The woman Eric had mistaken for Josie was wailing as she bashed him over the head again. From her stance Marla could see the large run in the woman's fishnet hose and the cheap clothes she wore were stained and torn.

Marla glanced at the large man prostrate on the floor at her feet. Up close he didn't look a thing like Aaron. This man had to be in his fifties and several strands of gray lightened the man's dark hair. How could Eric have made such a mistake? "What do we do?"

Geri cupped her hand over her mouth and shouted for Marla to stay out of the way. "If you get hurt, Eric will have my hide."

Marla signaled she would stay well away from the hysterical woman with the lethal purse. Several men attempted to interfere, but one direct hit from the leather bag stopped them in their place. Marla was afraid Eric would suffer brain damage if Geri didn't get to him quickly.

Another fight broke out between two men and one of the clerks was blowing a whistle trying to get everyone's attention. Geri was surveying the woman, trying to judge the best way to render her harmless when Marla noticed a police car pull up out front. Great, just what they needed!

"Geri!" she shouted, making her way past the two pugilists. "The police are here!"

Geri uttered a phrase that turned the air blue and shrugged her shoulders in a helpless gesture. "Sorry, lady."

With that brief apology she planted her fist in the woman's jaw and held out her arms to catch her as she fell to the ground. "Whew, no wonder."

"No wonder, what?" Marla asked as she helped Geri lower the woman gently down onto the tile floor.

"No wonder she's acting like this, she's plastered." Geri sniffed the woman's breath again. "From the looks of things, Ralphie-boy here is gonna be mighty grateful Eric put a stop to this little ceremony."

Marla cast a glance at the large man, noticing first

the business man's suit and then the large gold band on his left ring finger. "I think he's already married."

"Probably," Geri grunted as she began dragging the unconscious Eric down the hallway. "Grab a leg and let's get the hell out of here, Princess."

Marla hooked her purse over her shoulder and bent down to grab both of Eric's ankles. "Ugh, he weighs a ton."

"Yeah, but it's a nicely put-together ton." Geri grinned as they hefted him through the back door and into the alley.

Marla had to agree with that assessment. Even with his hair hanging in his face and that purple shirt wrapped up under his arms, Eric was adorable. Marla could hear the police barging through the front door just as the door closed behind her. "Will they come out here?"

"Probably," Geri said, and they half carried, half dragged Eric behind the large beige trash dumpster. "Get down."

Marla immediately ducked her head just as an officer peeped out the back door, checking the alley for any escapees.

Geri held a finger up to her pursed lips to signal Marla to keep quiet. The seconds dragged by, and as Marla's adrenaline slowed, she became more aware of their surroundings.

The sun was beating down on the dumpster, causing a pungent aroma to permeate the air all around them and she could swear she heard the scurrying of little feet. The policeman stepped into the alley and Marla knew that if any furry little creature chose that particular moment to try to get acquainted, she would be extremely verbal in her response.

Luckily there were no vermin poking around that particular trash can and the officer went back into the building without discovering their hiding place.

"Thank goodness." Geri exhaled the breath she had been holding.

Eric moaned and both women turned to face him. From the bruise coloring his jawline, old Ralphie-boy must have gotten at least one crack at him before going down.

"Eric," Marla whispered, still worried about being discovered. "Wake up."

"Come on, Pook, shake it off," Geri ordered, and Eric's eyes popped open.

"I told you to quit calling me that," he grumbled.

"It speaks." Geri chose to ignore his warning. "Think you can get to your feet?"

"Hell, yes." Eric started to sit up and groaned against the tidal wave of pain the slight motion caused in his head. "What happened."

"You went charging after the guy you thought was Aaron." Geri pried his eyelids open and studied his pupils. "Come on, you're all right."

Geri stood and brushed the dirt off her jeans. "We'd better get out of here before those people in there round up a lynch mob and come after you. I don't think they appreciated your interference on their wedding day."

Eric managed to prop himself up on one elbow and tried an experimental wiggle of his jaw. "Dang, that guy had a right like Mike Tyson. All I did was put my hand on his shoulder and the next thing I knew he was coming at me."

"I'd say he had imbibed rather freely over the past few hours," Geri informed him, as the two women helped him to stand on somewhat wobbly legs. "From the looks of things he made a soul connection with one of our more colorful tourist attractions and decided to make the arrangement permanent. I'd say he's got a wife somewhere who probably doesn't deserve such a paragon of virtue.''

The three of them made their way down the alley and around the corner of the street, still teeming with police cars and raving couples.

''You two wait here.'' Geri held up her hand. ''I'll get the truck and swing around the block. For Pete's sake, keep him out of sight. All we need is for one of those women to recognize him and start pointing fingers.''

''Gotcha.'' Marla flashed a thumbs-up sign and clamped her hand firmly on Eric's elbow when he would have argued. ''You've done enough, so just shut up.''

''Now wait a minute . . .'' Eric sputtered.

''If you start another scene and get thrown in jail, you will rot in there before either one of us lifts a finger to help,'' Geri threatened, and one glance at the tilt of Marla's chin confirmed it.

''Okay, okay,'' Eric surrendered and sat on the curb. ''Go get that monstrosity you call a pickup and I'll sit here like a good little boy.''

''Cheer up, Pook, I'm leaving you Marla for company.'' Geri flashed a smile that most women would kill for and trotted down the street.

Marla eased herself down on the curb next to him. ''Are you feeling better?''

''No, I feel like the entire company of *A Chorus Line* just danced the finale on my face.'' He winced as a taxi blared its horn at them. ''Guess the curb isn't the best place to sit, huh?''

''Probably not,'' Marla agreed, and they rose to walk side by side down the sidewalk. ''Is there anything I can do?''

"For what?" he asked, his attention captured by the sunlight shimmering off Marla's hair. He could smell her shampoo, and knew if he touched her hair right now, it would be warm from the sunlight and her body heat.

"For your face?" She stopped to glance up at him.

"You mean like kiss it and make it better?" he teased and was rewarded with that blush he had come to love.

"No, I meant like get you some ice or a wet rag." Her voice trailed off as she noticed a woman standing on the corner staring at Eric. Marla recognized her from the license bureau and realized she would be able to recognize Eric if they got any closer.

Eric stopped when Marla tugged on his arm. He noticed the trouble clouding her eyes. "What?"

"Kiss me," she ordered, tugging on the bright-purple shirt and turning him to face her.

"Excuse me?"

"I said, kiss me, dammit," Marla repeated. "Now!"

Eric didn't need to be told three times. He immediately slipped his arms around Marla's waist and brought his mouth down on hers. The initial pain he felt upon contact gradually gave way to an intense pleasure.

Marla was stiff and unyielding at first, but as his tongue crept out to tease hers, she softened in his arms and flowed against him. A small groan echoed from her and he pressed her closer against him forgetting they were standing on a street corner in downtown Las Vegas in broad daylight.

"I do like it when you take command," he growled against her throat and earned a similar response from her. "I just wish you would have picked some other place to try and make up."

"I was not attempting to make up, I was trying to keep that woman from recognizing you and calling the police." She pointed toward the corner.

Eric peered over his shoulder. "What woman?"

Marla struggled to see around Eric. "There was a woman standing there staring at you. I swear."

"I believe you, baby," Eric agreed, attempting to pacify the temper he saw flaring behind those eyes still dreamy with the lingering effects of his kiss.

"No you don't." Marla argued anyway. "But that's fine. I know she was there, and, hopefully, she didn't recognize you."

Eric tightened his arms when she attempted to step back. "I hope she comes back."

Whatever remark she had been about to make died a quick death as she lost herself in the sensual promise in his voice.

"Come on you two, shake a leg," Geri ordered, pulling up next to the curb. "Eric, get rid of that shirt. You stand out like a sore thumb in that thing."

Marla crawled in the middle of the cab and waited for Eric to climb in next to her. She hadn't registered the implications of Eric getting rid of his shirt, but as his bare arm came down around her shoulders and pulled her close to him she was faced with the heady sensation of having all that gorgeous bare skin next to her.

She thought about last night and how she had pressed her own skin next to his. Eric choked back a cough as she reached one finger up to barely caress the bronzed skin stretched over his pectoral muscle.

Marla jerked her finger away from the quivering skin and forced her eyes to the road in front of them. Geri's driving seemed to have gotten worse, and Eric was forced to hold Marla tightly to keep her from sliding all over the front seat. Her insides tightened each time Eric's arm pulled her closer, and she was grateful for the thick knit of the sweater that kept the tight buds of her unbound breasts from being visible. "Where are we going?"

"The strip," Geri informed, and swung the pickup into the parking lot of Caesar's Palace. "I'll take one side and you two take the other."

"We don't have any idea where the chapels are," Eric pointed out as Geri shuffled through a mess of papers that had been shoved into the glove compartment.

"Amateurs." She grinned and handed Marla a hastily scribbled list. "Here are the casinos with chapels and on the back is a list of independent chapels. When you go in," she advised, "let Marla do the talking."

"But . . ."

"No buts," Geri ordered. "You can't control your temper. Marla, you tell them that you are supposed to be a bridesmaid for your best friend but you've lost the name of the wedding chapel. Try to be convincing."

"No problem," Marla promised. "Where can we find him a shirt?"

Geri's eyes widened in surprise. "You're kidding, right?"

Marla felt a bit foolish as she realized that in a tourist town like Vegas there would be a T-shirt shop on every corner. Not to mention the numerous boutiques housed within the casinos themselves. "What about in there?"

Geri cast a glance at the impressive building in front of them. "Depends on how much you want to pay. There's a whole mess of designer shops inside."

"I'm not wearing another T-shirt," Eric stated, recalling the amused stares his natural gas shirt had drawn.

"Okay, you wait here and we'll run in and pick out something for you." Geri slid an unopened packet of cigarettes into her shirt pocket. "Give me some money."

Eric fished his wallet out of his back pocket and ignoring Geri's outstretched hand, placed several bills in Marla's lap. "You pick it out."

Geri's bottom lip stuck out in a mock pout. "Why, Pook, don't you trust me?"

"With my life, yes." His eyes narrowed, but a dimple played in his left cheek. "With my wardrobe, no way."

"No guts," Geri teased, walking away from the pickup, her braid bouncing with each long stride. "Come on, Princess."

"Princess?" Eric's eyebrows shot up and he grabbed Marla's hand to keep her from sliding away from him.

"Never mind." Startling herself as well as Eric, she leaned over and kissed him. Eric started to pull her more fully into his embrace, but she broke away and hurried after Geri.

"Well, hell." Eric grinned as he watched the two women walk side by side into the hotel completely unaware of the heads they turned.

He leaned his head back against the seat and closed his eyes. It wasn't even noon yet, but the lack of sleep was beginning to erode his stamina. He needed his wits about him if he was going to find Aaron and stop him from making a mistake. He would have to be in top form if he was going to be able to convince Aaron that marriage would be the worst possible action he could take right now.

Marriage meant compromise, responsibility, and a whole bunch of other rotten stuff that slipped his mind due to sleep deprivation. But he knew there were hundreds of good reasons for getting married . . . No, that wasn't right, he struggled to hold his eyes open, there were hundreds of reasons . . .

NINE

"We better get cracking if we want to find them."
Eric adjusted the sleeves of his new white silk shirt.

Marla had momentarily forgotten their misguided
mission and her spirits drooped considerably. She
wished there was some way to convince Eric of the
foolishness of their quest, but she knew it would take
more than a few well-placed kisses or well-meaning
words.

Eric joined the women in the parking lot and held
his hand over his eyes to help shade the reflections of
the car windows around them. "Give me the list."

Marla thought about telling Eric that she had lost the
paper, but that wouldn't stop him, so she slipped the
paper out of her purse and handed it to him.

"Hope you find what you're looking for, Pook."
Geri waved and trotted off across the busy street. Marla
watched her until she disappeared through the large
glass doors of the casino across the street.

Marla wondered if Eric had picked up on Geri's
words. She hadn't wished him luck in finding his
brother, but only in what he was looking for. The prob-

lem was, as Marla saw it, Eric didn't really know what he was looking for any more than she did.

"Let's go." Eric stuffed the paper into the pocket of his new shirt and grabbed Marla's hand before taking off at a brisk walk down the street.

Marla gazed at the large hotels and casinos lining the boulevard. "I thought the strip was downtown by City Hall."

"Those casinos were here first, but as the industry grew, the other casinos started stringing down Las Vegas Boulevard." Eric indicated the large street. "The strip is great, but wait until you see downtown tonight. The lights are so bright on Fremont Street at night that half the time you don't even need a flash for your camera."

"Will we still be here tonight?" The question slipped out before Marla could stop it, and she could have bitten her tongue off.

The light that momentarily brightened Eric's eyes was extinguished and the all-too-familiar scowl was back in place. "Depends on what happens after we find them."

Eric picked up his pace and Marla jogged to keep up with him. "What do you think will happen?"

"World War III," Eric predicted, and held the door of a large hotel open for her.

A young girl at the information booth inside the casino directed them to the wedding chapel on the second floor. Marla couldn't take the time to catch her breath or look around the casino since Eric was hauling her up the stairs.

"You're supposed to do the talking, remember."

Marla jerked her arm from Eric's ironlike hold. "Would you quit ordering me around like I'm a poodle!"

"Sorry."

"Stow it, Pook." It worked for Geri, she might as well give it a try. "Just get out of my way and let me do what I'm supposed to, okay?"

Eric's eyes narrowed at the use of his hated nickname, but he remained silent. For now.

A young blond woman was seated at a receptionist's desk slitting an envelope with open with her two-inch-long red fingernails. "Can I help you?"

"I hope so," Marla gushed with just the right amount of hysteria. "My best friend, Josie, is getting married today. She called me last night and told the name of the chapel and I can't remember it. I'm supposed to be her bridesmaid."

Marla could have been a fly on the wall for all the attention the blonde paid her. Her eyes hadn't left Eric since he had stepped into the room. "What's your friend's name again?"

"Josie Crandall," Marla supplied, wondering how that hussy would feel with those red talons stapled to the desk.

Eric sat down on the edge of the desk and gifted the receptionist with a dazzling smile. Marla thought she might throw up if she had to watch much more of the woman's blatant invitation. "It might be under the groom's name, Aaron Westbrook."

"And you are?" the blonde cooed.

A dead man, Marla thought.

"Eric Westbrook." He took the blonde's offered hand and held it in his own. "Aaron is my brother. When Marla called me about the wedding I just assumed she knew the name of the chapel."

Eric's tone of voice made Marla sound like she was a simple-minded twit. He would pay for this, Marla seethed.

The blonde cast Marla a glance that said she concurred with Eric's assessment of Marla's mentality before beaming up at Eric. "Let me check our reservations."

A red nail trailed down a partially made-out column in her appointment book. "I don't have anything for Crandall or Westbrook and we're booked up until five o'clock."

"Well, I guess this isn't the place," Eric sighed. "Thanks for all your help."

"If I can do anything else, let me know." The blonde filled her enormous lungs with enough air to make sure anyone within a twelve-mile radius could have the privilege of watching them pop over the top of her skintight dress.

Marla was already halfway down the stairs, so she didn't hear Eric's reply. How could he have sat there and let that woman ogle him like that? Was that the type of woman he really wanted?

She glanced down. She had always thought her bust was more than adequate, but after seeing Boom-Boom in there she felt like puberty missed her altogether.

"Wait up," Eric hollered after her "What's your problem?"

Marla glanced over her shoulder and kept walking. *What's your problem?* How dare he ask her what her problem was! Any idiot would know what her problem was. Jealousy was what her problem was, and it made her even madder that he didn't realize it.

"Look, if you want to go back and play patty-cake with Boom-Boom, fine." She stopped at the bottom of the stairs. "Just give me the list, and I'll take it from here."

If there had been a light bulb over Eric's head it would have lit up like the Fourth of July. As it was, he made do with a thousand-watt smile. Marla was jealous. "Boom-Boom?"

"Well, what would you call her?" Marla huffed.

"Blessed." He rolled his eyes heavenward and sighed.

Eric and Marla spent the rest of the afternoon questioning unsuspecting secretaries and clergymen to no avail. No one had ever heard of Aaron or Josie and most of the chapels didn't require reservations.

"This is it." Eric slid his pen along the last name on the list before tucking it back into his shirt pocket. "After this we'll contact Geri and see if she's had any luck."

Marla stepped into the parlor of the Haven of Bliss Wedding Chapel and sighed. "I don't believe it. Not one slot machine in sight."

Eric chuckled, recalling how shocked Marla had been to find the one-armed bandits in everything from bathrooms to grocery stores. "No neon, either."

Marla studied the plain white walls and elegant stained-glass arch at the end of the aisle and decided if her mother had to get married in Las Vegas, this place wouldn't be too bad.

Once Eric closed the door behind them they could hear the soft piped-in music. The orchestral rendition of "Close to You" was at once sentimental and comforting. Only the carefully printed price board listing the different wedding packages was out of place.

Eric tapped her on the shoulder and she noticed a woman shuffling her way down the white satin runner that lay between the white wicker chairs on either side of the main aisle. She was the picture of a grandmother, and Marla felt instantly at ease.

The woman inched her way down the aisle, straightening the pew markers as she came closer to them. "How can I help you, folks?"

Marla smiled at the woman, taking in the gray hair tightly woven into a bun at the base of her neck, the red crocheted sweater wrapped around her shoulders, the baggy support hose, and the . . . bright-yellow high-topped sneakers. Marla looked into those twinkling blue eyes and knew she couldn't lie to this woman. "I'm looking for my mother."

Eric started at Marla's words. He was prepared for her bridesmaid speech, and when she spoke the truth, it caught him unaware. "We think she might have made a reservation here for today."

Fatigue and the numerous denials had taken their toll on Marla and she was hard-pressed to keep from pouring out her heart to the woman. "She called me yesterday and told me she was on her way to Las Vegas to get married. I've tried every chapel in town. You're my last hope."

She's good, Eric conceded as he heard Marla add just the right touch of emotion to her words. She had the woman eating out of her hand.

"What's your name, honey?" The older woman took Marla by the hand and led her back down the aisle toward a small office.

"Marla."

"Well, Marla, you just let Frances take care of you." The woman motioned for Eric to follow them. "What was your mother's name, honey?"

"Josie Crandall." Marla sniffed, and Eric handed her his handkerchief.

"Oh, my," Frances said, and shot Eric a pained smile.

"You've obviously heard the name." Eric had been content to stay out of the conversation but now he stepped around Marla to confront the older woman. "I'm sorry, I didn't catch your name."

"I'm Frances." She held out her free hand to Eric. "And you are?"

"Eric Westbrook, ma'am." Eric was surprised at the firm grip on the old lady. "I'm looking for my brother."

"Um hum." Frances narrowed her blue eyes at Eric and frowned. "They called here all right. Yesterday afternoon. Ordered the deluxe wedding package."

"Then they were here?" Marla didn't try to keep the hopefulness out of her voice. She hoped they had already come and gone.

"Didn't say that." Frances opened the door to the office and wiggled her way around several stacks of boxes on the floor. "We're going through some old files and the place is a mess."

"Did they make a reservation?" Eric plastered a smile on his face, but he wished Frances would get it in gear and tell them what they wanted to know.

"Sure did," Frances said, and offered them a cookie out of a teddy-bear cookie jar.

"Thank goodness." Marla sighed and reached for one of the peanut butter delights Frances offered.

"Don't get your hopes up, honey," Frances cautioned, and munched on her cookie. "They called back this afternoon and canceled. Said they were gonna wait until they settled things with some family back in New Mexico. You two wouldn't be trying to stop 'em, would you?"

"No, ma'am," Marla answered truthfully. "I just wanted to be with my mother when she got married."

You've got to hand it to her, Eric thought as he watched the interchange between the two women. She hadn't batted an eye when she told that preposterous lie. "We'd better get going. Thank you for your time, Frances."

"You know," Frances began, ignoring Eric's attempts to leave, "I figure the reason we have so many divorces in this country is 'cause people won't leave well enough alone. You've always got some well-meanin' relative tryin' to stick his nose where it don't belong."

"You may be right about that," Marla agreed and edged her way out of the office. "I do appreciate your help."

"Anytime." Frances waved. "I'll even give you two a discount if you decide you want to tie the knot before heading back to New Mexico."

"We'll remember that." Eric grinned and wrapped his arm tightly around Marla's waist as he led her out of the little chapel and into the waning sunlight. "Well, that's a relief."

"Don't you feel even a little bit guilty about all of our interference?" Marla asked as they headed back down the boulevard toward Caesar's Palace.

"Sure," Eric admitted. "But that doesn't mean I don't have to do what's right and stop Aaron from making a mistake."

"How do you know it would be a mistake?" Marla wasn't going to let him off the hook that easily. "Maybe you don't know what's right in this case. Maybe marrying my mom is the best thing for Aaron."

Eric noticed the way Marla's eyes kept straying to the signs advertising shrimp cocktails. One of the great things about Vegas was the fact you could grab a shrimp cocktail and nibble on it as you strolled down the street.

He placed his hand on the small of her back and led

her into the nearest casino. "I thought you agreed with me about this marriage?"

Marla had been in so many casinos that day she couldn't have told one from another if her life depended on it. She didn't notice the tourists beginning to crowd into the gaming rooms, or the lounge acts warming up the before dinner crowd. She did notice Eric was leading them to a counter boasting ninety-nine-cent shrimp cocktails. "I did, but not now."

Eric held up two fingers to the man behind the counter and dug a couple of dollars out of his pants pocket. "What happened to change your mind?"

Marla took the large plastic cup filled with plump boiled shrimp swimming in a tangy red sauce and plunged her fork into the center to spear a large morsel. *I fell in love with you,* she wanted to say, even though she knew that would be the worst possible thing she could do. She wasn't ready to admit it and Eric certainly wasn't ready to hear it. Instead, she filled him in on another little truth she had discovered about herself. "I'm tired of running other people's lives. I want to take care of me for a change. I've decided to let my mother grow up."

Eric watched the way her face lit up as she bit into the shrimp. Her tongue slipped out to lick the sauce off her lips and he groaned. He had forgotten what exquisite torture it was to watch Marla eat.

"I'm sorry you don't agree with me." Marla couldn't help the smile that curved her lips. She had heard Eric's groan and knew exactly what caused it. She couldn't resist trying it again, and as her tongue swept across her bottom lip, she was rewarded by another agonized whimper from Eric.

"Aaron has always depended on me to make the important decisions for him." Eric led her across the busy intersection leading to Caesar's. "I can't just turn my back on him now."

"Let me ask you something . . ." She dug down to the bottom of her cup for the last shrimp. "Did you know about my mother before they decided to get married?"

"No," Eric admitted, and replaced her empty cup with his full one.

"Well, I didn't know anything about Aaron, either." Marla swirled her fork through the sauce, scooping another shrimp into her mouth. "What would you have done if you had known?"

"I would have put a stop to it."

"Exactly!" Marla punctuated the air with her fork. "I would have done the same thing and Mother knew it. The point is, they didn't want us to make this decision for them. Face it, Eric, our babies have grown up."

Eric tossed the empty cup into a nearby trash can. "I don't see how you can do a complete about-face like this. Last week you were just as against this marriage as I was."

Marla shrugged as they came up to Geri's pickup. She leaned against the side of the truck and faced Eric. "Maybe I've learned a few things about myself this last week. I don't know. I do know that they need our support right now rather than our derision."

"Support!" Eric flung his hands in the air and stared up at the security light above them. "Not only does she want me to condone this fiasco, now she wants me to help them along!"

"Would you hush?" Marla tugged on his arm. "People will think you've lost your mind."

"I have," Eric insisted. "That's the only reason I'm standing here listening to this sentimental garbage."

"It's not garbage!"

"Oh, excuse me." Eric bent over in a mock bow. "I'm sure you've come to the conclusion that this marriage is right out of the fairy tales. Well, didn't anybody ever tell you it doesn't happen like that in real life. In real life there is no happy ever after. Marriages break up, people leave, people die."

Marla's anger died as she heard the hurt in Eric's words. He didn't realize how much of himself he had revealed with his little passionate outburst. "Eric, now is not the time for this discussion. We are both tired and angry."

Some perverted part of Eric wanted to continue the fight. Wanted to push her as far away from him as she would go. If she went away, then he wouldn't have to face these strange feelings he was experiencing. He could tuck them away and only bring them out to examine as a distant memory. "You're right. I'm sorry. Let's forget about the whole thing and go find Geri."

"How are we supposed to find her?" Marla's eyes took in the scene around her. Now that the sun was down, she was witnessing Las Vegas Boulevard firsthand. Lights of every color twinkled, blinked, flickered, and glared their message. Her eyes moved from one neon lure to another, and she shook her head.

Eric's anger dissipated watching Marla's eyes light up. There wasn't anything stopping them from having one fabulous night together. He would show her Las Vegas and leave her with a perfect memory for the time he no longer had a reason to be in her life. "I'll go into the hotel and page her. You wait here."

Marla watched him jog off before fiddling with the handle of the tailgate. She managed to find the catch and lower the back of the pickup so she could sit down. Her feet ached from all the miles she had walked that day and she leaned against the side of the pickup so she could prop them up. She could hear the constant chatter of the people on the street around her as they began their journey into the wonder of the Strip. Couples strolled arm in arm, occasionally stealing a kiss. Familie's with wide-eyed children headed for the video arcades.

Marla felt a pang of envy as she watched the people around her fill their lives with a few hours of pure unadulterated fun. Had there ever been a time in her life when she had done that? Just done something for fun? No.

Well, tonight's the night, she decided. For one night she was going to act like there was no tomorrow. No Josie, Aaron, and Baby to deal with. No job hassles. No worrying what everyone around her was thinking or if she was going to bring shame on the Crandall name.

Just for tonight, she was going to be exactly what she was. A twenty-seven-year-old woman in love for the first time in her life.

TEN

Eric felt like James Bond as he watched the two women walk ahead of him into the casino. They turned to wait for him, each taking an arm. "Geri, I can't get over the change."

"Don't get used to it, Pook," Geri warned through her delicately painted lips. "This is all right every once in a while, but this bra thing is about to drive me crazy. Not to mention these panty hose Marla made me wear."

Marla hadn't believed that Geri had never worn panty hose until the other woman had ruined four pair trying to get them on. She finally put them on Geri herself. That had been an experience. "Oh, hush, you look fabulous. Doesn't she, Eric?"

"You both do," Eric agreed, and tried to pry his eyes off the wide expanse of ivory skin exposed by Marla's top. The first thing he wanted to do when he saw her in that silky red jumpsuit was fling her over his shoulder and carry her into his bedroom. The second was to make her wear something else. He spent the entire night alternating between fits of jealousy when other men looked at her and trying to keep his hands off her.

Dinner had been a new experience in torture as he watched Marla sample and lick and swoon as the delicious flavors blended on her tongue. The meal cost over three hundred dollars and he couldn't remember one thing he had eaten, although after watching the pleasure on Marla's face as she had experienced new dishes and tastes, he definitely felt like he had gotten his money's worth.

He had never known anyone who could throw themselves into a meal with such delight before. It was a side of Marla he hadn't expected. But then he hadn't expected her to come out of that bedroom half dressed or wink at him when she caught him staring at her barely concealed breasts. If he didn't know better, he would think she was trying to seduce him.

Geri insisted they take Marla to one of the floor shows that had made Las Vegas famous, and both women ignored Eric's groan of protest. The enormous room was more than half full, which Marla thought unusual for a Sunday night in the middle of January.

"You should see this place during a Friday or Saturday night. Almost everyone who comes to Vegas takes in at least one of the shows," Geri explained as the waiter placed a bucket of champagne on the table in front of her, "This is one of the most popular."

Eric quickly filled their glasses with the domestic champagne that came with the price of their tickets. "A toast to the two most beautiful women in town."

"Only in town?" Marla teased, and Geri threw back her head and laughed.

Eric was saved a reply as the house lights dimmed and the stage lights came up to signal the show was beginning. It had been several years since he had taken the time to see any of the shows and he found himself looking forward to the acts. The opening number started with several chorus girls strutting around the stage in elaborate feather headdresses and little else.

"They're naked," Marla whispered, tugging on Eric's arm in her urgency. "They don't have any tops on."

"Really." Eric pretended amazement. "Gosh!"

Marla realized how innocent she sounded, and forced herself to relax. "Well, you could have warned me."

"That would have taken all the fun out of it," Eric whispered in her ear.

Geri explained the show was done in the tradition of the floor shows in Paris. Marla wondered if that was supposed to make it art. Sort of like the difference between an old master's painting and the centerfold in some girlie magazine.

The show was compiled of various acts ranging from orangutans to acrobats bouncing up and down stair steps on their heads. Marla didn't know if it was her decision to have fun or the four glasses of champagne Eric had poured for her, but she was having a ball.

Once she noticed a pregnant woman making her way down the aisle and she thought briefly of her mother, but she quickly pushed any disturbing thoughts to the back of her mind to be dealt with tomorrow. She was beginning to like Scarlett O'Hara's philosophy of life. It was much easier to promise to think about it tomorrow.

After the show the three of them made their way into the central gambling area. Since Marla had never gambled before, the logic of blackjack and poker eluded her and she decided to stick with the slot machines.

"I'm going to hit the crap table," Geri informed them and sashayed her way through the throng to one of the tables surrounded with people screaming at a pair of rolling dice.

Eric handed a skimpily dressed woman a twenty-dollar bill and she handed him a cup and a roll of quarters. "Here, start with this."

Marla watched as his long, supple fingers broke the paper band on the quarters and shook them into her cup. "This ought to last me all night."

Eric didn't dispute her, knowing she would have to discover the addiction of the slots for herself. "Well, if you run out, I'll get you some more."

Eric led them to a row of quarter machines and explained the procedure to Marla. "Don't forget to keep tabs on the credit light."

"I thought the money just fell out when you won," Marla said, disappointed.

"It does on some machines," Eric explained patiently. "On some of them, though, the machine just tallies your winnings and holds them as credit. Once you've built up some credit you can push this button and the machine will automatically use your credits to play. When you want to get your winnings, push this other button and the money will fall out into the bin."

"Got it," Marla assured him and dropped three quarters into the slot before pulling on the lever that sent the lemons and oranges twirling. She got two lemons and a cherry. "Darn, that was close."

Eric watched as she plunked the rest of her quarters into the machine. She won a couple of dollars every few plays, but after about fifteen minutes she had depleted her supply of quarters. The look on her face was priceless as she stuck her hand into the now-empty cup.

"Oh my gosh." She raised startled eyes to Eric. "How did I do that?"

"It's easy, baby." Eric signaled for more change

and another young woman appeared with another roll of quarters.

"Eric, I can't let you give me any more money," Marla protested, digging through her purse.

Eric pulled her hand out of the bag and held it to his lips. "Don't worry about it. I want to do it."

"I don't know."

His eyes burned into hers as he turned her hand over and kissed the center of her palm. "Please."

"Okay." Marla agreed, not really remembering what she was agreeing to. He could have just suggested they stroll down the strip buck-naked and she would have said yes.

"How you guys doin'?" Geri hurried up next to them, flinging an arm around both of their shoulders.

"I lost twenty dollars worth of quarters," Marla confessed.

"You're doin' pretty good." Geri reached into the tiny gold bag Marla had bought her to go with the flashy gold harem outfit. "Let's head for the Golden Nugget. Marla needs to get a load of downtown."

Marla watched Geri take her chips to the bank to be changed into money and was amazed at the stack of bills the cashier placed in her hand. "How much did you win?"

"Two thousand." Geri shrugged.

"Two thousand dollars?" Marla jerked to a halt, causing Eric to bump into her. "You won two thousand dollars in only the few minutes you were gone?"

"It's the luck of the roll," Geri quipped, but Marla caught the delight hidden in the depths of Geri's green eyes.

Geri managed to maneuver her pickup onto the crowded boulevard and they inched their way toward downtown. Marla hoped she didn't look as awed as she felt at watching the sights around her. Even in the new clothes Marla had purchased for her new friend, clothes Geri professed were not her style, Geri still exuded a confidence Marla could only dream about.

Downtown was every bit as impressive as Eric promised. Thousands of lights held back the night and Marla could understand how people lost track of time in the casinos. With the bright lights to hide the darkness and no clocks on the walls to remind them of the time, people often gambled away the entire night, thinking it was only around midnight or one o'clock.

"I'm going to spend one quarter in every casino," Marla stated firmly. She had been appalled at how easily twenty dollars slipped away. No wonder so many people had a problem with compulsive gambling. Every time she pulled the lever she had just *known* she would win the jackpot!

Geri led them into the elegant Golden Nugget and showed them around. She knew several of the dealers and finally convinced Marla to try her hand at blackjack, and after a few hands she had an idea of how the game was played.

Eric slid out of the elegant dinner jacket he had purchased that afternoon and slung it on the back of his chair. He steadily lost money as his mind lingered on the way Marla fingered the growing pile of chips in front of her. He wanted those fingers to caress him the way they had the other night. He wanted to feel them trail down his back as he covered her with his body and made her truly his. He wanted to feel them tighten on him as he brought her closer.

"Eric?" Marla felt rather than heard the change in Eric's breathing and turned her head to study him. "Do you feel all right? Your face is flushed and your eyes look glazed. Maybe we should go back to the hotel."

"I think it's the lack of sleep," he offered as an excuse to the knowing eyes of the dealer. The man had given Marla a thorough perusing when they sat down, and he didn't blame Eric one bit for wanting to get to a hotel.

"You can change your chips at the cashier's window," the dealer informed Marla, who looked down at the stack of brightly colored chips in front of her.

"Did I win?" she asked in surprise. She hadn't been paying much attention to the chips the dealer slid her way. Eric had been too close and she had been concentrating too hard on the way he smelled, the way he occasionally brushed his hand over her silk-covered arm.

"Yes, ma'am." The dealer grinned and pointed to the cashier's cage.

Geri had wandered off to find another crap table and Eric went to find her while Marla went to collect her winnings. He hoped to convince her to stay and let them take a taxi back to Caesar's. He could feel the tension building between him and Marla and he didn't want Geri running interference.

"Hi, Pook." Geri grinned as she held her fist over the green felt-covered table and shook the dice. "Go, baby!"

Eric watched the required numbers come up on the dice. The crowd around the table went wild. He patted Geri on the back. "Looks like you just can't lose tonight."

Geri winked before picking up the dice again. "That's a bunch of bull. I could be flat broke in thirty minutes and we both know it."

That's Geri, Eric thought. She might give the appearance of having been caught up in the thrill of victory, but she was smart enough to know when to stop. She didn't find much time for the casinos, but when she did try her luck, she never varied from her game plan. She always had a set amount of money to lose. When that was gone—she quit.

"We're heading back to the hotel," Eric hollered over the noise that erupted after another winning throw. "Marla's exhausted."

"Yeah, sure, tell me another one, Romeo." Geri's grin had a hard edge to it. "I like her, Pook. I like her a lot."

Eric heard the thinly veiled warning in Geri's words and echoed it with his own. "I do, too."

Geri winked at the admission. "I wondered how long it would take you to figure that out."

"What do you mean?" Eric didn't like being the last one to know his own feelings. How had Geri known he was crazy about Marla? Did it show? Did Marla know about it, too? Did the two women discuss him behind his back?

Geri watched the storm brewing in those dark eyes and shook her head. "Don't worry so much. Just be sure you treat her right."

"Hey, I thought I was your friend," Eric grumbled.

"You are," Geri assured him, rattling the dice. "I just don't want to see you screw this up."

"Oh, throw your dice." Eric waved. "I'll call you in the morning before we head home."

Geri waved back, but her mind was already back on the challenge in front of her.

Marla was waiting for him by the front door looking like the cat that had swallowed the canary. "Guess how much I won! Just guess!"

Eric helped her out onto the street and began searching for a taxi. "I have no idea. Twenty bucks."

"Not hardly." She sniffed at his guess and reached

into her purse to pull a wad of bills out and wave it under his nose. "I won two hundred and fifteen dollars."

"That's great, but I don't think you ought to be flashing it around." Eric tucked the money back in her purse and pulled her up against him. "You never know how some people might react to seeing that much money being waved around. I'd hate to have to chase some purse snatcher down the street in these new shoes."

"Oh," Marla said, feeling foolish. She knew better than to wave money around in a crowd. It was just the thrill of actually winning it. "Sorry."

Eric leaned down and kissed the top of her head, taking a second to breathe in the scent of her perfume. "Your hair smells good."

Marla self-consciously raised her hand to finger the curls that had captured his attention as he led her toward the taxi pulling up to the curb. The ride to the hotel was filled with momentary bursts of conversation followed by long tension-filled periods of silence. Marla's relief at seeing the driveway of the hotel was such that she actually sighed out loud.

"Are you tired?" Eric asked as they made their way through the lobby toward the elevators.

"Yes," Marla admitted, noticing the disappointment in his eyes. "I thought you were feeling bad. Did you want to go somewhere else?"

Thousands of thoughts forced their way into Marla's consciousness. Did he want to go back to Geri? Had she been so successful in her transformation that Eric now found Geri desirable? Did he want to go find a stranger to spend the night with? Or was it that he just didn't want to spend another second with her?

"Look, I can find my way," Marla insisted as they

boarded the elevator. "If you want to go back to the casino, please go."

"I never said I wanted to go anywhere," Eric said, pushing the button that would take them to the fourth floor. "What's the matter with you?"

"Nothing is the matter with me." Marla crossed her arms around her waist and turned to study her reflection in the mirrored wall of the elevator.

"The hell there isn't," Eric argued, taking her by the shoulders and turning her to face him. "One minute you're fine and the next you're trying to push me out the door."

"I was not."

Once inside the room, Marla realized they would be spending the entire night together. Without Geri.

"Would you tell me what's wrong?" The confusion in Eric's voice was clear. He had serious plans for this evening and they did not include having another damned argument! "What did I do?"

Slipping out of her new shoes, Marla settled on the arm of the couch and rubbed her aching toes. "I just don't want you to feel like you have to babysit me. I understand if you would rather go find some . . ."

Eric flung his jacket down on the couch, and his tie and shirt quickly followed. "That does it!"

Eric quickly covered the space between them, placing his hands on her shoulders and forcing her to look at him. "I am exactly where I want to be and you are precisely who I want to be with, although this is *not* what I want to be doing!"

Marla's insecurity fell away as she gazed at Eric's nude chest rising and falling with each labored breath. The smooth skin of his shoulders cried out for her touch, as did the heat of his eyes. He did want her, Marla realized with a shock. He didn't want Geri or

Boom-Boom or some stranger. He wanted her, and the knowledge made her heady with power.

"Would you tell me what the heck is going on here?" Eric demanded, taking a step closer. "I thought we were getting along fine and then you go and pull some mysterious woman trick to make me think I'm losing my mind."

"I don't know what you're talking about." She reached up and placed her hands on his chest, her fingers caressing the smooth skin she found there.

Eric looked down at her hands resting on his chest, watching them as they leisurely made their way from the flat plane of his stomach up to massage the tense muscles of his neck. He shook his head. "Weren't we arguing just a minute ago?"

Marla tilted her eyes up to his and shook her head. "I don't remember."

"How can you not . . ." Eric's breath left his lungs and hard shudders wracked his body as he watched the tip of her tongue peek out to slide along his skin.

Power! She now knew the meaning of the word, and it was an experience to be savored and tested. She skimmed her tongue along his heated skin until she came in contact with his flat male nipple. Recalling how his lips had wrung cries of pleasure from her, she tried an experimental nibble.

She was rewarded with a tortured moan from deep within his chest. She flicked the tip of her tongue over the nipple and he jerked in her arms before lifting her against his chest and carrying her to the bedroom.

She felt a momentary twinge of panic as he took control from her, but she realized this was what she wanted, what she had wanted from the moment she had seen him in that gondola, and she gave herself over to the feeling. Just for tonight, a tiny voice whispered in her head. Or forever, another voice beckoned from her heart.

Eric prayed Marla knew what she was doing because there was no way he would be able to stop now. It hadn't taken but a second for him to find the zipper that ran the length of her back and slide it down. It had been impossible for her to wear anything underneath the top of the jumpsuit, and once he peeled the silk from her shoulders she was completely exposed to him. "Ah, baby, you are so beautiful."

Marla finally managed to find the zipper of his black pants and lower it. Her fingers brushed over his arousal and she jerked her hand back. "Don't stop now, sweetheart." Eric chuckled at her shyness but didn't force the issue. With time she would become more confident, more daring, he was sure of it. He busied himself with slipping her clothes the rest of the way off, stopping to caress or taste each inch of skin as he exposed it. He loved how each new sensation he brought to her seemed like the first. She cried out his name and went rigid in his arms as his fingers explored her.

Fearing that she might pull away from him again, he didn't allow her the chance. Instead, he immediately began a new assault on her, shocked when she responded with fresh passion and renewed energy. "Hold on, honey," he urged, taking his place between her legs. "Let's do it together this time."

She was incapable of muttering anything more than a few incoherent moans as she writhed under his manipulations. Her body ached and she didn't know how to appease it.

Heat flared through her limbs making them quiver as she wriggled, making room for him, allowing him full access to her. "Eric."

His name was a keening wail on her lips and he

knew that he had to have her. Now. He felt her beneath him and surged. "Marla."

It had been a long time since Marla had been with a man, not since her one disastrous affair in college. She felt a mild discomfort as Eric eased his way into her heated flesh, but it was quickly replaced with a new sensation. A feeling of such utter completeness that she cried out loud with the rightness of it. This was where she belonged, where she would always belong. In this man's arms, close to his heart.

Eric felt her stiffen under him and cry out. Had she reached fulfillment so quickly? "Are you okay?"

"Yes," she whispered against his throat. "It's wonderful."

"You'll get no argument from me." He agreed and slowly resumed the pace of his lovemaking.

She caught his rhythm and within seconds they both reached the outer edge of paradise before drifting down together in a sweet liquid fog of passion-induced sleep.

Eric heard Marla mumble something as he rolled off her and tucked her under his arm to lie beside him, but sleep overtook him before he could decipher her words. Strange, but they sounded like I love you.

Marla awoke with the awkward sensation of not knowing where she was. She knew it wasn't her room or her bed. Then with the clarity of fine crystal, she knew.

She could feel Eric's warmth along her backside, as they had been sleeping spoon-fashion. A smile curved her lips at the thought. She had always wondered what it would feel like to sleep cupped together with another person, and she discovered she rather liked the sensation.

Since Eric's arm was wrapped around her waist, holding her firmly against him, she doubted she could get up without waking him. Embarrassed by the memory of her behavior last night, Marla decided to try to fake sleep until Eric arose and left.

"Oh, no, you don't." Eric's words were a soft rumble in her ear. "I've been waiting for hours for you to open those beautiful eyes."

Conscious of her morning breath, she refused to face him and kept her eyes to the wall in front of her. "Why were you waiting?"

"For this." He turned her in his arms and kissed her, dragon breath and all. "You were incredible last night, lady."

"Uh, thank you," Marla stammered. She hadn't thought they would have to talk about it. Jason, her boyfriend in college, never even held her afterward. This was uncharted territory and she hoped she wouldn't bungle it. "You were fine, too."

"Fine?" Eric's eyebrows wiggled over eyes alight with mischief. "I guess I'll have to see if I can't improve my rating."

"No," Marla protested as the meaning of his words sunk in. "You were great, fantastic, unbelievable.

"Eric, you have to stop." Marla batted his seeking hands away.

"Why?" He looked like a little boy who had just been told he couldn't have dessert.

"Because," Marla rolled her eyes and flushed to the roots of her hair, "I have to go to the ladies' room."

"Oh." Eric did a certain amount of blushing himself and released her. "Don't be long."

Since she didn't have any idea how to answer him, she grabbed her robe off the floor and scurried toward the bathroom.

Once behind the relative safety of the solid oak door, she let out the breath she had been holding. Her reflection stared back at her and she raised a trembling hand to lips still swollen from Eric's kisses.

She trailed her hand down her neck and gently skimmed over her tender breasts before stopping to lightly massage her lower abdomen. Yes, she could feel a difference in every part of her Eric had touched.

She winced at the soreness between her legs and headed for the bathtub and a long, hot soak. Surely Eric would get the message when she didn't come back out and leave. She wanted to be back in full armor before she had to face him again. Last night had been a beautiful memory for her to store within her heart, a treasure to be taken out occasionally and remembered.

Today was a different story. Today she went back to being plain old Marla Crandall—practical, level-headed . . .

No, she would never be that Marla Crandall again. She was caught between the two worlds she had created. She wasn't the hard-nosed business woman she had always tried to project, nor was she the gallivanting good-time girl of last night.

Today she would start on a new journey of discovery to find out who the real Marla Crandall was. It was a scary but exciting thought, finding this new person. She hoped she was up to the challenge.

Eric had almost drifted back to sleep when he heard the bathwater running. That little minx, he grinned, and shot off the bed only to find the bathroom door locked. What kind of game was she playing?

If she thought she could spend last night in his arms and then just dismiss him like so much excess baggage, she had another think coming. He knew last night had been good for her. Surely she didn't doubt the effect their lovemaking had on him! He had been extremely verbal in his delight, calling her name over and over as she took him places he had never explored before.

Her passion had been contagious, and they had both been captured by the intensity of their emotions. She had wept in his arms and he held her against his heart all night. He had never done that before, never even wanted to. Usually he was out the door well before the light of day.

Eric gave the doorknob a vicious twist, but it held firm. He turned back toward the bed and began rummaging through the sheets for his clothes.

She was in love with him. There was no other explanation for last night. Marla might be beautiful, but she was first and foremost the most practical woman he had ever known.

It hadn't taken him long to realize that she hadn't been with a man in a long time and he supposed it was natural that she was feeling a little . . . A little what? Upset? Disappointed?

Had she not found the same ecstasy in his arms that he had found in hers? Did she expect something else from him?

Marriage! Surely not, knowing the way they both thought about that subject. She made it clear she wasn't interested in a permanent relationship right now. Of course, she also declared her mother to be crazy with the same breath.

She was no longer claiming her mother had lost touch with reality. In fact, she was now firmly ensconced in her mother's corner. Did her change of heart also include her own feelings on marriage?

Of course, Eric deduced, slapping his forehead with the palm of his hand. It was a reverse empty-nest syndrome. Her mother would no longer be relying on Marla to take care of her, and Marla was afraid of being alone. She was looking for someone to replace Josie. Well, it wasn't going to be him.

He forgot about his missing underwear and strode naked through the living room to his bedroom. If Ms. Marla Crandall thought she was going to trap this man just by going to bed with him, she was a fool.

Marla could hear the water running in Eric's bathroom and decided it was safe to leave the confines of the bathroom. She had stayed in the hot water long enough for her skin to begin to pucker and she quickly dried off on one of the large fluffy towels on the heated towel rack.

The bath helped the soreness of her body, but it hadn't done a thing for the ache in her heart. How could she go out there and face Eric.

She quickly slid into the jeans and top she had packed in her haste and fluffed her bangs out of her swollen eyes with her fingertips. Her body wasn't used to all this physical activity and she longed to crawl back into the bed and sleep for the next twenty-four hours.

Some carefully applied makeup helped cover a multitude of sins, and she prayed Eric wouldn't be his usual observant self today. Or if he did notice the purple smudges under her red-rimmed eyes, he would be gentleman enough not to make any comment.

She spotted the phone on the nightstand next to her bed and decided to call her mother. Eric had tried twice last night, but there hadn't been any answer at her mother's. He finally called an employee and asked the man to drive over to Aaron's cabin, and the man had called back to report that no one was there, either.

Marla read the dialing instructions on the phone and

quickly punched the numbers that should connect her with her mother. "Mom?"

"Marla?" Josie had picked up the phone before the first ring had finished. "Marla, where are you?"

"I'm in Las Vegas. Where did you think I would be after that late-night phone call?" Marla sank onto the edge of the bed and bit her lip to keep from crying. She never allowed her mother to see her troubles, believing she had to be strong, but now she longed to pour her heart into the phone and let Josie offer her some words of advice for once.

"Is Eric with you?" Josie asked with what sounded suspiciously like a sniffle.

"With *me*?" Did her mother suspect what had happened between the two of them last night?

"In Las Vegas," Josie clarified. "Did you two go up together?"

"Yes," Marla sighed, and hoped her mother didn't hear her relief through the phone. "He was bringing me home from dinner when Aaron called and insisted on flying up here right away. We spent the entire day yesterday going from one chapel to another trying to find you."

"I can't believe you would do something like that, Marla." Josie's sniffles were more distinct now.

"Mom, if you'd just let me explain." Marla tried, but Josie refused to listen and broke the connection. When Marla tried the number again, there was no answer. "Great."

A sharp knock on her bedroom door reminded Marla that she had more pressing matters to deal with than her mother. "Yes?"

"Do you want anything to eat?" Eric asked through the door.

"I'll have whatever you're having." It seemed like

a safe enough answer, but from Eric's reaction, she had just asked for the Hope Diamond.

"I'm having a nervous breakdown," he bellowed. "But please feel free to join me."

Marla waited a minute until she was sure Eric must have left the suite before she ventured out of her room.

"I had begun to think you were going to hide in there all day," Eric said from the doorway of his bedroom.

"Eric!" Marla spun around, her hand flying to her throat. "You scared the life out of me."

"What's the matter, Marla?" Eric closed the distance between them with two long strides. "Did you think I'd left?"

"I thought you must have gone to breakfast." She hoped she didn't sound as nervous as she felt. Even the thought of breakfast had her stomach flipping over.

"No, I thought we might as well get this over with first." Eric led her gently but firmly by the arm and helped her sit on the couch.

"Get *what* over with?" She crossed her legs at the knee and clasped both hands together in her lap.

"Don't." His whisper was more threatening than any shout could ever have been. "You told me one time to quit playing games. Well, I've quit. Please do me the same courtesy."

"All right."

"Still making me pull those teeth, I see." Eric leaned back against the couch, his knee barely brushing hers as he turned to face her. "Do you want to tell me what last night was all about?"

Marla shrugged indifferently, but the threat of tears was very real. "I don't know what you mean."

"Can you tell me what you expected to come from last night?" Just how clear did he need to make this.

Marla raised tear-filled eyes to his and shook her head. "I don't know."

"Oh, come off it, Marla." Eric stood up to pace the floor in front of her. "A woman like you doesn't do anything without a well-thought-out game plan. What was it? Cheap thrills? An education? Marriage?"

"Stop it!" Marla ordered. "Just stop it. You have no right to talk to me like this. I really didn't think—"

"That's the truth," he interrupted. "You didn't think. As a matter of fact, neither one of us did a great deal of thinking last night."

Marla's head ached from lack of sleep, and she simply was not up to this conversation. Eric had evidently concocted some explanation for her behavior and nothing she could say or do would convince him otherwise. "Just believe whatever you want, Eric."

"I want to believe the truth, if you think you're capable of telling it." His words were sharp, revealing his frustration.

"All right." Marla rose from the couch and stepped inside her bedroom to lift her bag off the end of the bed. "The truth is, I wanted to have one night of memories. One night of feeling free to do whatever I wanted and damn the consequences. I didn't tell you about my lack of experience because I was afraid you would make a big deal of it."

"It *was* a big deal!" Eric exploded. "If I had known, I could have made it better for you."

"If it had been any better I couldn't have survived." She tried to smile, but her heart ached too deeply. "Don't feel guilty, and for Pete's sake, don't think I expect you to marry me because of it. This is the 1990's not the 1890's. I knew I would have to pay for it today, but I had it. I had my one night of freedom and I'm not sorry, Eric, not one little bit.''

Eric watched her heft the bag onto her shoulder and stroll out the door without ever looking back. She had already stepped into the elevator before he realized just how big a jackass he had been.

His started to go after her and tell her he had made a fool of himself, but his pride held him rooted to the floor. What could he say to her anyway that would make up for the accusations he had flung at her?

It would be better to give her some time to cool off. She probably needed to walk around for a while. When she came back they could sit down and talk like reasonable adults. He wouldn't yell at her or jump to erroneous conclusions.

Yeah, that would be the right thing to do. He'd just order some breakfast and she would probably be back by the time he finished with his coffee. Or at least by lunch. He was out the door at twelve-o-four.

He searched the casino, the restaurants, and the boutiques. No Marla. He asked the desk clerk, the cashier, the doorman. No Marla. She must have left the hotel. He started on one side of the street and made his way back up the other. No Marla. Never once did it occur to him that in a town the size of Las Vegas she could have walked right past him and he wouldn't have noticed.

By two o'clock he had calmed down enough to allow his mind to work on a less emotional level. Jamming his fists into the front pockets of his jeans, he stalked back to the hotel. It was time to call for help.

Boris answered on the first ring and told him Geri hadn't made it into the office yet. "I thought she must be with you."

"No, I left her at the Golden Nugget around eleven

last night.'' Eric picked up the phone and took it with him as he walked to the large window of the suite and stared down at the city below him. Now he had to find two women in that maze of streets. Impossible. Eric gave Boris a list of numbers where Geri could leave a message when she came in.

"Of course." Boris sounded offended that Eric doubted his abilities to assess the situation and come to the proper conclusion.

"Thanks." Eric pressed his finger on the disconnect button and immediately called down to the desk to see if Marla or Geri had left a message.

"Yes, sir," the desk clerk informed him. "I have three messages for you."

"Give them to me." Eric lowered himself onto the edge of the bed and searched through the nightstand drawer for a pencil and paper.

"I have a message from a Mr. Aaron Westbrook. You are to call him at the ski lodge." Eric could hear the shuffling of paper over the phone and pictured the woman flipping through her notes.

"Got it." Eric wrote Aaron's name on the hotel stationery.

"Then I have a message from a Marla Crandall."

"Yes?"

"It was delivered in a sealed envelope, sir, and I'm not allowed to open it." The woman said he would have to come to the desk and pick it up.

"Fine, I'll be right down for it." Eric started to hang up the phone when the woman asked him if he wanted his other message. "Go ahead."

"It's from a Geri Halifax. It says . . . Oh, dear." The woman gasped.

"It says what?" Eric muttered, although he had a pretty good idea what it said.

"It's pretty graphic sir. Maybe you should pick this one up also."

If Geri had talked to Marla, Eric had a pretty good idea what the note said, and he didn't blame the woman for not wanting to read it out loud. "I'll be right down. Have my bill ready."

"Yes, sir," the desk clerk assured him, clearly relieved at having been given a reprieve from his pornographic mail.

It took Eric less than a minute to stuff his new suit into his travel bag and head out of the suite. He told himself he had taken that swing through Marla's room to make sure she hadn't forgotten anything. It had nothing to do with the fact that he could still smell her perfume in the air and in his mind's eye he could clearly see her stretched out on that large bed next to him. There was nothing productive at all about that line of thinking.

The clerk handed him a bill and the notes as soon as he stepped up to the desk. Since he had already given them his credit card, all that was required was a signature. "Can I get a taxi out front?"

"Yes, sir." The clerk smiled and handed him his receipt. "Just tell the doorman."

The doorman assured Eric a taxi would be arriving within the next few minutes. Eric took the time to read Marla's note.

Eric,
  I am going home. I need some time to think.
                                             Marla

He crumpled the note into his fist and shoved it into his pocket. What kind of game was she playing now?

He flipped open the note from Geri and grimaced at the blunt language slashed across the page. No wonder the clerk hadn't wanted to read it. It was a wonder the paper didn't go up in flames.

In typical Geri fashion she had hit the nail right on the head. He was a lousy son of a bitch.

ELEVEN

"I gotta stop," Geri said, whipping the pickup into the parking lot of a small convenience store just inside the city limits of a tiny New Mexico village. "You need anything?"

"No, thank you." Marla shook her head and resumed the straight-ahead stare she had perfected over the last few hours since leaving Las Vegas. And Eric.

Geri muttered something Marla was sure she didn't want to understand and slammed the door shut. Marla managed to smile as Geri strode into the store and demanded a pack of cigarettes. She had been searching every nook and cranny of the pickup for the last half hour, forcing Marla out of her thoughts with irritating regularity.

Marla had bitten her tongue to keep from allowing her irritation to show. Geri was doing her a tremendous favor by driving her back home and she didn't want to damage their newfound friendship by pulling some broken-hearted lover routine.

Geri was examining the candy counter in an effort to stall returning to the morbid atmosphere prevailing in the pickup. She wished Marla would cry a little, or scream, or curse Eric to a life of jock itch. Anything would be better than sitting there like a stone statue.

When Marla called her from a phone booth inside the Circus Circus Hotel and explained she needed to get away from Eric, Geri had been more than glad to offer her help.

She told Marla to grab a taxi and meet her at the office. By the time Marla arrived, Geri had already booked her on the next flight to Albuquerque. Marla hadn't batted an eye, just said that would be fine. If it hadn't been for Boris and his keen eye, Geri would never have known Marla was terrified of flying.

Marla tried to deny it, even pointed out that she had flown with Eric. In the end, though, Boris had been able to convince Geri she should drive Marla home. It wasn't more than a few hours and she could spend the night with Marla before heading back the next day.

Marla bought the story about Geri needing a break and wanting to visit with Aaron. Geri and Boris both knew if Marla had suspected them of concocting the whole thing just to keep her from having to fly, she wouldn't have allowed it.

Now Geri wondered if driving had been such a good idea. Marla hadn't said ten words since they left Vegas and they still had a couple more hours on the road. Geri respected Marla's right to silence, though, and didn't try to get her to talk. She was dying to know exactly what Pook had done, but she wouldn't ask. If Marla wanted or needed to tell her, she would. Until then, Geri would allow her the dignity of suffering in silence. Even though it was driving her crazy.

"Here, I thought you could probably use a drink." Geri handed Marla a large soft drink and a candy bar. "The guy in there said there wasn't much in the way of restaurants in this town but not the next one has a Dairy Queen.''

"I'm not really hungry," Marla said, accepting the drink, but slipping the candy bar back into the sack.

"Maybe not, but I am," Geri stated, and wished she was a little better at being diplomatic. "You should probably try and eat a little something anyway."

Marla smiled at Geri's last remark, recognizing it as a peace offering for her harsh tone. "Okay, maybe some French fries."

"Yeah," Geri grinned, "and a double meat cheeseburger with the works and a chocolate shake so thick it bruises your throat trying to suck it up the straw."

As much as Marla relished the martyr image she was perfecting, she admitted Geri's idea of supper had its own appeal. "Maybe a small one."

"That's it," Geri said, lighting a cigarette with the lighter.

Marla watched the terrain become more familiar as they made their way deeper into New Mexico. Although she had been gone less than forty-eight hours, she found herself longing for her little apartment and the safety it would provide. She had never enjoyed long vacations even as a child, and two days was long enough for her to start missing her home.

The next town was only a few miles away, and when Geri pulled into the parking lot of the restaurant, Marla wanted to tell her to forget it. Instead, she followed Geri into the brightly lit building, and once the aroma of the food hit her, she realized how hungry she was. She hadn't eaten anything since Eric had taken them to dinner last night.

She availed herself of the rest-room facilities while they waited for their food and was appalled at the reflection in the mirror over the sink. Her eyes were red even though she hadn't shed a tear and her already pale complexion was a sickly gray. Her hair was sticking out at odd angles and she searched through her purse for her brush.

Feeling somewhat more presentable, she joined Geri, who was already digging into her food with relish. "That looks good."

"Mumph." Geri urged Marla to join her.

Marla found that once she managed to eat a bite of her cheeseburger, her body demanded more despite her depression, and she quickly emptied her plate. "This was a good idea. I was hungrier than I realized."

Geri swiped her remaining french fry through the puddle of ketchup on her plate and leaned back in the booth. "Nothing like a burger and fries."

"Geri, I want to thank you for doing all this for me . . ." Marla began.

"Would you hush," Geri cut her off. "I don't know what happened between you and Pook, but I do know it must have been serious for you to take off like this. What I do know is that you are my friend, and I always help my friends when I can."

"Eric is your friend," Marla pointed out.

"Pook didn't ask for my help." Geri shrugged. "Even if he had, I would have probably helped you anyway."

"Why?"

Geri motioned to her sloppy jeans and shirt. "I may not always look like a woman, but I *am* one. There comes a time when we women have to stick together."

"Oh." Marla felt the corners of her mouth tip up and she gave in to the grin. "I do like you, Geri Halifax."

"I like you too, Princess." Geri stretched and reached for the check, but Marla grabbed it away from her. "Hey!"

"Hey, nothing," Marla argued back. "You are making this little trip because of me and I'm going to pay for it."

"The hell you are!" Geri bellowed.

"The hell I am!" Marla bellowed right back and stalked to the cashier and handed her the money. "I'm sick and tired of people telling me what I can or cannot do. If I want to pay for this meal, I will."

"Yes, ma'am." Geri grinned and followed Marla out to the truck. "Am I allowed to continue driving or are you planning to take that away from me, too?"

Marla was in the process of opening the door on the driver's side of the truck before Geri's words sunk in. "Guess I got a little carried away."

"I don't know," Geri said, climbing behind the wheel. "I kind of liked that little show of backbone. You're going to need the practice if you're going to be with Eric."

"I'm not," Marla muttered, slipping back into her melancholy at the mention of Eric's name.

"Not what?" Geri pretended not to notice the change in Marla's voice.

"Not going to be with Eric. I don't think I should see him anymore." Marla heard the hesitation in her voice and wondered what to make of it. Surely it was better to make a clean break with Eric. They really didn't have a future. Did they?

"Why would you do a fool thing like that?" Geri whipped the truck around a large eighteen-wheeler, barely avoiding a head-on collision with another truck before slipping back into her lane.

Marla released her death-grip on the dashboard long enough to answer, "Because we fight too much. If I say yes, he says no. If I say up, he says down. And don't give me any of that opposites attract theory, I know that we're attracted to each other.''

"Then what's the problem?'' Geri cracked her window and lit a cigarette, dragging the acrid smoke into her lungs and exhaling out the window.

"The problem is, we're just not right for each other,'' Marla explained, wishing she had a vice to fall back on. "We're both too independent and set in our ways. If you expect to have a viable relationship, both parties have to be open to suggestion and compromise.''

"Are you talking about a love affair or a corporate merger?'' Geri shook her head. Having never been in love or involved in a serious relationship, she didn't feel right offering advice, but this was ridiculous. "Viable relationship?''

Marla admitted it did sound a little stuffy and realized she was backing away from her feelings by categorizing them into neat little departments to be dealt with the same way she dealt with stock options and mutual funds.

She had never been too keen on playing options due to the high risk involved. True, a client could make a lot of money in a hurry, but that same client stood to lose everything if the option turned out wrong. She always tried to steer her clients toward investments that would be safer in the long run.

She was doing the same thing with her feelings toward Eric. She wanted to invest her heart in Blue Chip stock rather than the riskier options. She wasn't interested in a short-term win-or-loss proposition. She wanted to have the security of the safe, long-term investment. Eric had been right. She did want marriage.

The realization that what she protested against all along was the very thing she desired was a hard pill to swallow. The harder realization was that she had all but made it impossible for her dreams to ever come to fruition. She assured Eric marriage was not on her agenda for the next few years on more than one occasion. She laid her ten-year plan out before him to examine and he had seen the wisdom of her strategy. She quoted him statistics and book-learned facts without one iota of firsthand knowledge and thought herself so clever. So in control of her emotions and her destiny.

She allowed her guard to slip with Eric because he assured her of his own revulsion with the state of marriage. He had been completely open concerning his opinion of relationships, telling her he was more than happy with his life as a bachelor. And heaven knew, she was aware of his feelings about women trying to trap a man into marriage.

He was sure her mother had gotten pregnant for that purpose. Just as he had evidently come to the conclusion Marla had slept with him with the same reason in mind.

"Sorry to interrupt," Geri's voice was unnaturally loud after the quiet of the last couple of hours. "I need directions."

Marla blinked into awareness and glanced at the familiar surroundings. "Sorry. I guess I blanked out there for a while."

"Only for the last two hours." Geri grinned and followed Marla's quietly spoken directions, pulling up in front of the tidy apartment complex within minutes. "Nice place. Maybe I should consider changing jobs."

"It's good to be home," Marla sighed, fitting her key into the door and swinging it open.

Safe. Had she actually thought she would be safe from Eric and his memory once she got home? She was reminded of how Eric had checked out her apartment for burglars after their first date. She could see him stalking from one room to another, checking in closets and under beds.

Remembering the state she had left her bedroom in, she hurried down the short hallway hoping to straighten some of the evidence before Geri's trained eye took in the rumpled bed and strewn clothes and drew the correct conclusion. "I'll be right back."

Geri heard the note of panic in Marla's voice and followed her to the bedroom. "Are you gonna be sick?"

Marla, caught in the act of picking her discarded panties off the edge of the bed, reddened under Geri's concerned stare. "No, I just didn't want you to see this mess."

Geri's green eyes swept across the room and grinned. "I would have picked you for a cleaning nut."

"I am," Marla admitted, hurriedly tossing her dirty clothes into the wicker hamper in the corner of the room. "I just left in a hurry and didn't have time to straighten things up."

"I promise not to look, if you'll point me in the direction of the little girl's room." Geri held up her right hand.

Marla pointed at the partially open door and winced as Geri was forced to step over her blouse and bra on the way.

Geri wasn't gone but a few minutes before she returned with one black sock dangling from her finger. "I must say you have strange taste in socks, Marla."

Marla felt her face flame as she gazed at Eric's lost sock. "Uh, I . . ."

"Never mind," Geri chuckled. "The look on your face tells me everything I want to know."

"Nothing happened!" Marla asserted, snatching the

offending sock from Geri's grasp and flinging it into the trash can.

"If you say so." Geri strolled into the kitchen before Marla could dig herself in any deeper. "Have you got anything to drink?"

"There's a bottle of wine in the back of the refrigerator." Marla could hear Geri shuffling through the leftover remains of the few meals she had eaten at home in the last two weeks. "Did you find it?"

Geri strolled into the bedroom with two plastic cups and the bottle of very domestic, very cheap wine. "I knew you were a woman after my own heart."

"How so?" Marla accepted the offered cup and took a sip of the ruby-red liquid.

"I can't stand that fancy stuff that has to be at room temperature and allowed to breathe. Give me a bottle with a screw top that costs $3.99 and I'm in heaven." Geri drained her cup and refilled it. "A toast. To two women who have seen the enemy and run like hell."

Marla didn't even pretend to be confused. She knew Geri was talking about the fact that Marla had run from her problems with Eric. "Sometimes victory can be found in retreat."

Geri raised her newly plucked eyebrow over her cup and both women sputtered their wine trying not to laugh. "You don't let me get away with anything, do you?"

Geri instantly refilled their glasses. "It's a habit you pick up in my line of work. After a while you learn to read through the bull and see the truth."

Marla settled onto the edge of her bed. "What truth do you see in me?"

Geri sat down next to a slightly tipsy Marla and grinned at the other woman's inability to handle the slight amount of alcohol she had imbibed. "I see a woman who gets drunk on three glasses of wine."

"Ah, but it's cheap wine," Marla insisted, as though that made all the difference.

"Well, one more ought to get you through tonight." Geri tipped the remainder of the wine into Marla's glass. "Only for tonight, though. Tomorrow you have to face the decisions you've made and deal with them sober."

"Sober," Marla whispered and lay back against the pillows she had so recently fluffed to eradicate the impression of Eric's head.

"That's a girl," Geri encouraged, watching Marla's eyes flutter and close. She took the empty cup from Marla's limp fingers and pulled the snowy-white comforter across the bed to cover her.

She had known it wouldn't take much of the wine, no matter how low the alcohol content, to put Marla out. The woman was exhausted from her ordeal with Eric followed by the intensive analyzing she had done on the way home.

Her body and mind both deserved a rest and Geri would make sure she got one. If her calculations were correct, Eric would be beating on the front door sometime before the night was over, and Geri was determined to keep him away from Marla. At least until she had been given the time to discover what it was she was feeling for Eric and what she wanted to do about it.

Geri made her way to the living room and the pillow-filled couch. This cupid business was harder than she expected, and if she wanted to see her two friends together, she would really have her work cut out for her.

*   *   *

Geri felt as if she had barely closed her eyes when she heard the pounding. Instantly awake, it took only a second to scan the area around her and find the source of the noise. Someone was pounding on the front door. Eric.

Pushing her hair out of her face, she made her way to the front odor. "Hold your horses, Pook, I'm coming."

"Geri?" Eric's voice came loud and clear through the front door.

"In the flesh." She grinned, opening the door and allowing him to enter.

"What are you doing here?" he demanded, his eyes searching the hallway for Marla.

"I brought her home after you screwed up," Geri answered quickly. "Keep your voice down, she's exhausted."

Eric couldn't keep a blush from creeping up his neck to stain his high cheekbones. He remembered the small amount of sleep he had allowed Marla the night before, and wondered if Geri was aware of what had transpired in that hotel room. "I need to see her."

"Why?" Geri fumbled in the pocket of her coat and located a cigarette. She slipped into the coat. "Come outside with me while I smoke this."

"Marla won't care if you smoke in here." Eric pointed to a large ashtray settled on the corner of one end table.

"I don't think you are in any position to tell me what Marla does or doesn't care about," Geri pointed out, and stepped onto the front porch.

"What did she tell you?" Eric asked, coming to lean against the railing beside Geri.

"Nothing." Geri flicked her ashes off the cigarette and watched them scatter in the slight breeze coming down from the mountain. "I didn't ask and she didn't offer."

"She must have told you something or you wouldn't have left me such a graphic message and you wouldn't have driven her home." Eric took the forgotten cigarette from her fingers and held it to his own lips. It had been a long time since he smoked his last cigarette, but his body hadn't forgotten the rush of nicotine.

"The hell I wouldn't have!" Geri snatched the cigarette out of his hands. "Once I saw her it didn't exactly take Sherlock Holmes to figure out you had pulled your usual stupid macho routine on her. She asked me to find her a way home and I did."

"You could have put her on a plane." Eric recalled his own lonely flight home. How he found himself sniffing the air for the scent of her perfume. How he glanced at the empty seat beside him and called himself a fool.

"Come on." Geri stubbed out her cigarette and grabbed Eric's hand. "Buy me a burger."

"It's almost midnight," Eric protested.

"So?" Geri didn't see the problem and headed for the sleek red Blazer parked at the curb. "Don't you have any place in this burg that stays open all night?"

"Of course." Eric didn't like the snobbery of the question. "Get in."

Geri hopped into the passenger side of the vehicle and tried to ascertain Eric's mood. He was edgy, anyone could see that, but there was something else. Some hidden feeling she didn't think he was even aware of yet. She had heard the desperation in his plea to see Marla, the sadness in his eyes. Man, if this was love, she was glad to have skipped that particular experience!

The restaurant was half full of people who weren't worried about the late hour. Truckers stopping for a few cups of much needed coffee and conversation. A group of bowlers who just finished their weekly exhibition. A few other late-night travelers.

Eric led her to the booth in the back corner away from any listeners. "Okay, tell me what's wrong?"

"Calm down, Pook." Geri reached across the table and patted his hand in a soothing gesture. "I know how you feel."

"You do?" Eric scowled and held his cup up for the waitress to fill with coffee. "How?"

"Okay, so maybe I don't know precisely how you feel," Geri admitted after ordering. "But I'm smart enough to see you're both hurting."

A subtle light crept into Eric's eyes. "Is Marla really upset?"

"You don't have to act so damned happy about it."

"I'm not happy," Eric insisted, but the corners of his mouth quivered with a suppressed grin. If Marla was really upset, maybe there was a chance they could work things out and forge some kind of relationship that would be beneficial for both of them. "Do you think she wants to see me?"

"Nope." Geri hated to watch that light flicker and die, but she didn't want him to get his hopes up just yet. "Maybe she will tomorrow, but not right now."

"You can convince her," Eric asserted. "I have faith in you."

"You and I need to have a little talk first." Geri ignored his scowl and reached for the ketchup. Only after she had liberally doused her french fries and burger did she look up. "What did you do to her?"

"Me!" Eric grabbed the bottle from her and drowned his own fries. "I didn't do a damned thing."

Geri saw the lie in his eyes and knew his conscience would force him to face the truth. "Okay."

"What's that supposed to mean?" Eric jabbed his fork into the pile of homemade fries on his plate. This conversation was not going according to his schedule.

"Nothing," Geri answered, the picture of innocence. "You said you didn't do anything, so I believe you. I mean, sure I like Marla, but you and I are practically family."

Eric chomped down so hard on his fork he reached up to make sure he hadn't broken off his front tooth in the collision. "Marla likes you, too."

Geri slid her empty cup across the table and replaced it with Eric's full one. He never noticed. "I guess she's pretty flighty, though, huh?"

Eric's eyes shot up from the river of ketchup he had been watching on Geri's plate. "Marla? No. She's the most practical woman I've ever known."

"Really?" Geri flipped her braid over her shoulder before it wound up in her ketchup. "Well, I thought she sounded pretty flaky. I mean, she just up and left you for no good reason this morning and then she didn't say anything about you at all on the ride here."

Eric concentrated on the piece of lettuce dangling from his hamburger bun, refusing to meet Geri's eyes. "Well, it's possible that I may have done something to upset her."

"Oh?" Geri leaned back, taking Eric's coffee cup with her.

"After last night I guess I expected her to start making some sort of demands on me."

Oh, this was getting good, Geri thought, and leaned forward to rest her elbows on the table. "Just exactly what did happen last night, Pook?"

Eric reached for the empty cup in front of him and

set it back on the table with a bang. "I'm sure you can figure it out."

Geri hooted and slapped her hand over her mouth when the other diners peered over the tops of their booths to see what was so funny. "You mean to tell me that just because she slept with you, you expected her to start making wedding plans?"

Eric flung his napkin on the table and reached for the ticket the waitress had placed on his side of the table. "It has happened before, you know. Look at the mess my brother is in."

"Pook, I hate to be the one to inform you of women's liberation," Geri deadpanned. "But a woman doesn't sleep with a man to get him to marry her anymore."

Eric counted out some bills and laid them on the table for a tip and grabbed Geri's elbow to lead her out of the restaurant filled with nosy people. "Then why does a woman sleep with a man?"

"Are you serious?" Geri squinted up at Eric's face.

"Yeah, I am." Eric led her to his Blazer and helped her inside.

Geri waited until they were headed back toward Marla's apartment before answering him. "Lots of reasons, I guess. Companionship, curiosity, fun."

Eric didn't particularly care for the list Geri was rattling off. "Why do you think Marla slept with me?"

"Hell, Eric why are you asking me these things?" Geri roared.

Eric grimaced at the rise in the decibel level. "Because you won't let me ask Marla?"

"How on earth am I supposed to know why she slept with you? You're a good-looking guy. Anybody can see she's crazy about you—"

"Are you sure?" Eric interrupted. Had Geri picked

up on the same vibrations he had? Did Geri's meaning of crazy equate with Marla's meaning of love? "You really think she cares about me?"

"I can't imagine why," Geri muttered as Eric slid into a parking space next to her pickup. "Jeez, Eric, why are you making such a big deal out of all this? It's not like you were her first or anything."

If Eric had been able to control his facial expressions as well as he controlled the rest of his body, he would have gotten away with it, but Geri caught the guilt flashing in the darkness of his eyes and flew at him.

"You didn't!" she shrieked, standing in the middle of the sidewalk. "Tell me you didn't."

"I didn't! I wasn't her first, but I have a feeling I was damned close to it," Eric offered as an excuse.

"I suppose that's what caused you to come to the brilliant conclusion that she was trying to trap you into marriage." Geri stormed off leaving him standing alone in the middle of the sidewalk with his guilt.

Eric caught up with her at Marla's front door. "What should I have thought?"

Geri realized she had forgotten to get a key to the apartment and flipped her pick set from her back pocket. "I don't know, Eric. Maybe she got tired of waiting. Maybe she wanted some cheap sex. Maybe she was doing a comparison study. Or maybe she just got caught up in the moment and went with it."

"Then you don't think she did it on purpose?" Eric asked, watching her deftly pick the lock on Marla's door and making a mental note to have Marla install better locks.

Geri turned around in the doorway and held her hand up to his chest to prevent him from entering. "I don't know why she did it. Maybe deep down she did think about marriage. We all do from time to time. I guess she just needs a little time to get over it.''

Eric didn't protest when Geri shut the door quietly in his face. He thought over what she said about Marla needing time to get over him and his stupid accusations and his heart ached. Okay, fine. He'd give her time. She had one month to come to her senses.

TWELVE

Who needs women? That's what Eric asked himself as he flopped back in his easy chair to watch the ball game. If he had a woman in his life, she would gripe about the amount of time he spent watching football on Sunday afternoons. She wouldn't let him sit around in his favorite sweat pants and drink beer. She wouldn't let him have a night out with the boys.

He refused to pay attention to the little voice in the back of his mind reminding him he didn't actually do any of these things now. The point was, he could do them if he wanted to. If he let some woman into his life, she wouldn't let him.

Aaron had left early this evening saying he needed to get back to work on a sculpture commissioned by an Oklahoma businessman. The man had picked Aaron more for his heritage than for his work, and Aaron wanted to present the man with a piece that would show both the Apache side of him as well as the artist. Eric knew Aaron hadn't gotten much work done during the last two weeks and he blamed Josie. The woman hadn't understood why Aaron wanted to wait to get married and thought that by threatening to stop seeing him, she would be able to force the issue.

Aaron had turned the tables on her instead. When Josie gave him the ultimatum about getting married, Aaron had finally seen her for what she was. Not that Aaron told him any of this. All Eric had been able to get out of his taciturn sibling was that they fought and decided it would be better to call the whole thing off. But Eric knew that his little brother finally recognized Josie for the little gold digger she was.

Just like her daughter, Eric thought, flipping the channel during half-time. When Marla realized Eric had no intention of being trapped into marriage, she had slunk away with her tail tucked in between her legs.

He silently chastised himself for thinking of Marla in such derogatory terms, but he knew it was the only way he could keep his vow to stay away from her. If he allowed himself to remember how caring and funny she could be, he would lose control and park himself on her doorstep.

It was a shock for him to realize he was capable of such desperation. He had never clung to the memory of a woman before and he found it unsettling the way his mind returned to time spent with Marla.

He couldn't ski Red Devil without recalling her daredevil recklessness. The sight of her brightly clad body shooting down the mountain and winding up under twenty pairs of skis would pop up and distract him. He forced himself to go to the restaurants they had gone to in an effort to steel his memory. But the sight of other women gobbling their food reminded him of how much pleasure he had received watching Marla enjoy every morsel she placed on her tongue. Once he thought about her tongue, he was a goner.

Money made him think about Marla. Dancing made

him think about Marla. Sleeping, walking, breathing made him think about Marla and it was driving him crazy.

So he developed his own personal smear campaign against her memory. Maybe if he told himself that she was a greedy little manipulator often enough, he would eventually start to believe it. He still had a week to go on his vow.

The score on the football game was so one-sided it would be next to impossible for his team to lose. He had no interest in watching the second half of the slaughter. He had no interest in the Sunday night movie or the wildlife show on PBS.

After walking a circle around his living room three times he admitted what he really wanted was to talk to Marla. He picked up the phone and dialed her number before he could change his mind. He almost dropped the receiver when she answered on the first ring.

"Hello?" Marla almost jumped out of her skin when the phone rang just as the detective was opening the creaking door of the supposedly haunted house. "Hello?"

"Marla?" Eric heard the tightness in his voice. He switched the receiver from his left hand to his right so that he could wipe his palm on the thigh of his jeans. "This is Eric."

"Yes, I know." She set her half-eaten dinner on the coffee table before she dropped it and hit the mute button on her remote control.

"How are you?" He tried to keep it formal. He didn't want her to realize just how hard this phone call had been for him.

"Fine. How are you?" What *do you want*? her mind screamed, but she was determined not to ask.

"I'm fine. How's your mother?" Eric hit the heel of

his hand against his forehead. He never had this much trouble talking to a woman.

"She doing fine. The doctor's said the amniocentesis showed there are no abnormalities and the baby should be just fine." Is this what he wanted? Was he calling for Aaron?

Damn, he thought, *is she going to make me pull teeth again?* "I'm glad to hear that."

"Are you?" She didn't try to hide her disbelief.

"Damn, Marla, what kind of man do you think I am?" Eric exploded. "Just because things didn't work out between our families doesn't mean I'm not concerned about the child."

Tears sprang to Marla's eyes and she swiped them away. She couldn't keep her voice from betraying her emotions, though. "I'm sorry, but you never cared about the baby before."

"Ah, don't cry, honey," Eric urged. He hadn't intended to make her cry. He wasn't exactly sure what he had intended, but it wasn't to make her cry. "I'm sorry. For everything."

What was that supposed to mean? Had he called to ask her forgiveness? Did he want to make up and continue as they were? Or did he want them to part friends? "I think we can divide the blame fairly evenly."

"Well, I'm not sure about that, but I do know I didn't mean for things to end the way they did." Hell, he hadn't meant for things to end at all.

"Yes, well, I suppose things never turn out the way we expect them to," Marla sighed into the phone, not caring if Eric heard the hurt in her words. "I wish things could have been different."

"Maybe they can be." She had given him a margin of hope, no matter how slim, and he grabbed it with both hands. "Could we have dinner next week?"

"Next week?" *What was wrong with tonight?* "I . . . Yes, I'd like that."

"Great. I'll pick you up after work on Monday." Eric's vow expired on Monday at midnight, but what were a few hours here or there? Not wanting to give her the chance to change her mind, he hurried the good-byes and hung up. For the next week he would make sure he was conveniently unavailable for Ms. Marla Crandall. She wasn't going to escape him this time.

"Marla, I can't get these pants on," Josie yelled from the bathroom. "See if I've got anything larger in my closet."

Marla dutifully checked through the numerous pairs of slacks hanging in her mother's closet. "I don't see anything, Mom. I guess it's time."

Josie came out of the bathroom with her pants un-zipped and a frown on her face. "I'm only in my fourth month, I didn't have to start wearing maternity clothes with you until I was in my sixth month."

"The doctor said this was normal, Mom. It doesn't mean you're having twins." Marla had been over this same argument for the past five days after Josie some-how managed to outgrow the majority of her pants overnight. "You've been running around all week with your pants unzipped. How long do you think you can keep that up?"

Josie held her breath and sucked in her stomach, trying the zipper one more time. It wouldn't budge. "You're right. Let's go shopping."

Marla tried to convince her mother to let her move back home and take care of the bills, but Josie was adamant. She insisted she would find some way to have this baby and pay her small debts. Luckily the house was paid for and all Josie owed were a few credit-card bills.

Marla lifted a pair of navy-blue maternity slacks to take to her mother who was shuffling through the dresses on the far side of the store. Josie hadn't wanted to even look in the overpriced maternity shop, but Marla insisted.

Driving by Sweet Expectations on her way to the office she had noticed several outfits much more suitable for her mother than the pink-and-blue confections they were likely to find at the discount store.

"Mother, you can't go around in a cotton-candy pinafore," Marla had argued, and Josie finally relented. Marla noticed Josie gave in easily these days. Being without Aaron had taken all the fight out of her once-spunky mother, and Marla was trying desperately to fill that empty space he left behind.

Josie was holding up a sophisticated knit dress that didn't have the appearance of a maternity garment at all. The soft green color was almost the exact same shade as her eyes. "What about this?"

"I love it," Marla stated emphatically. She knew from experience that keeping her mother's mind off her love life was for the best.

A saleswoman had been watching the exchange between mother and daughter and decided to make her presence known. "I've got that same dress in bright red," she said to Josie. "She would be stunning in red."

Marla watched her mother carefully. While the assumption that Marla was the pregnant one was certainly logical, Marla wondered how her mother would weather it.

"Yes, she *is* stunning in red." Josie grinned at

Marla. "But she's not the one who'll be wearing it, I am."

The saleswoman gracefully recovered her aplomb, sensing a sale, and congratulated Josie. "Then green is the one you want. I have another little dress over here that will take ten pounds off you."

"Great, I can wear that one for my doctor's appointment," Josie teased, and winked at Marla as if to say, "See I'm going to be all right."

By the time Josie was fixed up, Marla had ·spent over three hundred dollars. Thinking about her mother swirling in front of the mirror, her hands cupping the small mound in front of her, Marla knew it was money well spent. "Come on, I'll buy you lunch."

"Can we try that new Chinese place?" Josie asked, loading her sacks into Marla's car. "I'd kill for an egg roll."

"Cravings, huh?" Marla teased.

"No, just hungry."

The restaurant was busy and they had to wait for a few minutes before a table could be cleared. The aroma of cabbage and onions and ginger assaulted Marla's senses, and her mouth actually began to water. "This was a good idea, Mom."

"Can we go?" Josie asked in a small, tight voice. Her hand latched painfully onto Marla's.

"Mom, what's wrong?" Marla held Josie's cold hand in hers. "Are you hurting? Do you need to go to the doctor?"

"I just want to . . ." Josie's eyes glanced quickly to the corner booth and she pleaded, "Please, get me out of here."

"Sure, Mom." Marla told the waitress her mother wasn't feeling well and they wouldn't be needing a table. Just before the door closed, Marla caught a glimpse of Aaron's astonished face.

Her mother's desire to leave was clearly understandable considering Aaron was seated with another woman. Marla hadn't been able to see her face, but she couldn't help but notice the long black hair cascading down her back. That jerk! Her mother was walking around with his child in her womb and he had already found another woman. "For two cents, I'd march back in there and give him a piece of my mind."

Josie looked frantic. "No, Marla, please. I just want to go home."

Marla helped her mom into the car and stalked around to her side of the car, casting venomous glances at the restaurant.

"Marla, wait!" Eric burst out of the restaurant and strode quickly across the parking lot toward her.

Afraid her mother might hear what she had to say to this man, she closed her door and met him halfway. "What do you want?"

"Aaron sent me out here to ask about Josie," he explained although his eyes drank in every inch of her. "He noticed how quickly you left and was afraid there might be something wrong."

Heat shot through her veins, although if it was from anger or Eric's close proximity, she couldn't have said. She hadn't seen or heard from him in over a month, but her attraction to him was as strong as ever. "I'll tell you what's wrong. Your brother didn't even have the decency to wait until his child was born before he found some other poor unsuspecting woman to wield his charms on."

She had turned back toward her car, desperate to get away from Eric and the power he held over her, but his hand grabbed her elbow, spinning her back around to face him. "The woman sitting with us is my sister, Lanie. Aaron may be irresponsible, but he isn't cruel."

"Oh." Marla's anger died with her embarrassment.

Eric noticed she hadn't removed her arm from his hand, and he took advantage of the situation to pull her closer. "Why don't you and Josie come back in and say hello in person? Lanie is dying to meet you."

Marla jerked her attention away from the sensation his thumb was creating as he skimmed it along the inner flesh of her elbow. "She is?"

"Sure." He grinned at her surprise. "You know little sisters, she gets a kick out of teasing me about my women."

Marla's heart lurched at the plural form of the word. "How many *women* do you have running around?"

Despite her light tone, Eric clearly heard the worry behind her words. "Oh, maybe five or six."

"Five or six?" Her eyes shot up at the teasing in his voice.

"Or maybe just one," he whispered softly before bending his head down to place a gentle kiss on her lips. "But believe me, she's a handful."

"Marla!" Josie's plaintive wail shocked them both.

"Tell her that I'll call her later." Marla remembered her mother was still living under the misconception that Aaron was with another woman. "I need to get Mom home."

"Is she doing okay?" Eric asked, genuinely concerned.

"She's adjusting." Marla couldn't tell him she was okay. Any woman who cried herself to sleep every night could not be considered okay. "She is just easily upset right now. Hormones." Allowing him a quick kiss, she hurried to the car.

"What did he want?" Josie asked before Marla was halfway into the car.

"Aaron wanted to know how you were doing."

"Then why didn't he come out here and see for himself?" Josie huffed, and ran a protecting hand over her abdomen.

"I guess he thought it might make matters worse." Marla shrugged and headed the car toward her mother's home.

"What could be worse than seeing him with another woman." Josie sniffled and reached into her handbag for a tissue.

"It wasn't another woman, Mom, it was their sister Lanie," Marla explained, and nodded when Josie stared at her in confusion. "He wondered if we might ask her to lunch sometime next week. She has been staying with him and I think she's driving him crazy."

"That poor woman." Josie reached for another tissue. "Of course we'll call her. Just because her brothers are idiots doesn't mean she had to inherit the trait."

Marla took umbrage to her mother calling Eric an idiot. He might be an idiot, but it was up to her to voice the opinion. "I'm sure Lanie's very nice. I'll call her tonight and maybe we can meet somewhere tomorrow evening."

"Fine. Just as long as I don't have to see Aaron." Josie sniffled one last time just as they were pulling up in front of her house.

"Mom, don't you think it's time you called him?" Marla eased into the dreaded conversation.

"Why?" Josie's eyes filled with tears again. "There is nothing left to say."

"You still have to decide about custody rights," Marla reminded her gently. "Aaron will want to have time with the baby."

"I guess I can't deny him that." There was no bitterness in her voice. "He'll make a wonderful father."

"I'm beginning to think he'd make a pretty decent husband." Slipping off her red leather boots, she padded to the kitchen and filled the bright-yellow enamel kettle with water. "How about some hot chocolate?"

"I wonder if I was so concerned about having people say the same things about me all over again that I pushed Aaron away so he wouldn't have to suffer from the gossip." Josie remarked later in front of the fire.

"The circumstances are not the same at all, Mom." Marla had tried to reassure her. "It's not like you're sixteen."

"No, I'm forty-four and he's thirty," Josie had declared as if Marla was unaware of the age difference. "Not only will people say I trapped him into marriage, they'll call me a cradle robber!"

"Mother, would you stop it!" Marla implored before her mother went off on another crying jag. "I thought you and Aaron had already worked out the age thing. I honestly don't think anyone would pay much attention to it."

"You did." Josie whispered the accusation.

"That's because I'm your daughter, not some stranger on the street," Marla fired back. "Now hush up."

"All right," Josie chuckled, "Just remember, you have to be nice to me tomorrow night."

"I'm still not sure about this whole Lamaze thing," Marla moaned.

"But I need you," Josie beseeched, and Marla gave in. She would be her mother's birthing coach, but she wouldn't like it.

"Okay, coaches, I want you help the mother relax," the Lamaze teacher instructed. "Make sure she doesn't breathe too fast or she will hyperventilate. Keep talking to her in a soft voice. Give her gentle commands.''

Marla shifted to allow her mother to rest more comfortably on the pillow at her back. She wrapped her arms around Josie's expanding waist and practiced the circular massage. "Come on, Mom, relax. Don't tense up against the pain. Breathe it through. Deep, cleansing breath. That's good.''

"Very good, Marla,'' Mrs. Avery, the instructor, commented as she strolled amid the couples stretched out on the floor. "Don't *ask* the mother to breathe or relax, *tell* her gently but firmly.''

One of the husbands growled the orders at his wife and everyone laughed. Marla had been worried about looking out of place in the class, but out of the seven couples in their group, only four of the mothers had their husbands as a coach.

Besides Marla and Josie, one woman had her best friend as a coach and a young unmarried girl had her mother. They were a diverse group to say the least.

"Okay, that's all the exercises we'll learn tonight,'' the instructor told them, and everyone began helping the mothers off the floor. "Take a quick break and then I want you to watch a film on childbirth to help you prepare for the experience.''

"Can I be excused? I've already witnessed the experience firsthand?'' Josie teased, patting Marla on the head.

"No, Josie, being knocked unconscious does not count,'' Mrs. Avery answered back.

Marla allowed all the expectant mothers to use the rest room first and the film had already started by the time she slid into her seat.

"This film will take you through the entire pregnancy.'' Mrs. Avery said. She continued her dialogue through each frame, explaining each step from the actual discovery, through buying supplies, and finally the onset of labor. "Everyone's labor is different. There are certain signs to watch for."

"Such as?" one of the husbands asked, pen at the ready.

"Such as when the baby drops into position. Some women claim they experience an overabundance of energy a few days before going into labor. You might experience false labor pains for a few days before the actual contractions begin."

"How will we know the difference?"

"You'll know!" Josie exclaimed along with Mrs. Avery.

"This part of the film shows the beginning of labor," Mrs. Avery informed them and everyone turned their attention back to the competent woman on the screen. Marla wondered if the woman would take off her carefully applied makeup for the delivery.

"Once they've determined the contractions are close enough, they will go to the hospital and meet their doctor."

The film was an actual account of the woman's labor as well as the birth. Marla had been watching the film and listening to the comments with her trained logical mind, but when she saw the doctor pull the baby out and place it on the mother's stomach, her insides twisted and she barely made it to the bathroom in time.

"Marla, honey, are you okay?" Josie asked, trying to peek under the stall door.

"I'm fine," Marla said, leaning against the door. "I'll be out in a minute."

Marla could hear the water running, and in a few minutes a wet paper towel appeared over the door. "Here, take this."

"I don't know what came over me," Marla apologized. "I've never had a weak stomach before."

"Don't worry about it, sweetie," Josie soothed. "Don and Jason hit the door right after you."

The fact that two of the other coaches had also been nauseated by the sight helped ease her embarrassment considerably. "At least I won't be alone in my shame."

"Honey, there's nothing to be ashamed of," Josie countered. "If you want to know the truth, my stomach was churning a little bit, too."

"Yeah, but you didn't go rushing down the hallway."

"Honey, I don't rush anywhere anymore," Josie said on the way back to class.

Marla barely heard what her mother was saying. She could have sworn she saw Aaron peeking through the doorway at the end of the hall.

What was he doing? Spying? "I'll be right back, Mom."

"Don't be long." Josie assumed that Marla needed a little fresh air to clear her head and didn't insist on going with her.

Marla hurried down the hospital corridor, hoping to catch Aaron lurking on the other side. When she flung open the door, the other hallway was empty. She headed for the main entrance, and only after she stepped into the frigid air did she remember the two feet of new snow on the ground. Aaron couldn't possibly have made it down the mountain until after the roads were plowed.

The class was over by the time she made it back, and she had to stand around and take a good ribbing along with Don and Jason.

"Just hope they don't do that during the actual delivery," Mrs. Avery teased. "Josie, I'll see you in the morning. Is Marla coming with you?"

"Coming where?" Marla asked.

"I'm having an ultrasound in the morning," Josie explained. "It's just routine."

Marla looked to Mrs. Avery for confirmation. "She's telling the truth. Dr. Reynolds likes to do an ultrasound at four months to make sure everything is proceeding normally. I just thought you might like to come along and see the baby."

"You can see the baby?"

"Sure." Mrs. Avery gathered her papers and the three women strolled down the hallway together. One of the couples always stayed behind to make sure that Mrs. Avery didn't have to walk out to her car alone. "And by this time it almost looks like a baby."

"Can they tell whether it's a boy or a girl?" Marla asked, amazed she was going to be able to see the tiny life growing inside her mother.

"Not really. Sometimes they'll make an educated guess, but I can't tell you how many times a couple has been assured they're having a boy only to find their newborn doesn't have outdoor plumbing," the nurse cautioned. "Besides, your mother already told Dr. Reynolds she didn't want to know. Will you be coming?"

"I wouldn't miss it," Marla declared, and took her mother's hand to help her down the icy steps.

"Marla, you don't have to come with me," Josie protested over hot chocolate later that evening.

"But I want to come." Marla used her spoon to push her marshmallow under the rich brown liquid. "Although it really ought to be Aaron going with you."

For the first time in weeks her mother didn't dispute Aaron's right to be a part of the baby's life. "I wish he would."

Marla's cup hung halfway to her lips. "Do you want me to call him?"

Josie shook her head and tears highlighted the sadness in her eyes. "He doesn't have a phone, remember. Besides, if he really wanted to be with me, he would have contacted me weeks ago."

"Mother, he *has* contacted you." Marla reminded.

"Through me. Heck, he even called Pris down at the restaurant to check up on you. Why won't you at least talk to him?"

"What good would it do?" Josie shook her head. "Eric hasn't changed his mind, and Aaron can't stand the thought of ruining his relationship with his brother."

"Don't be so hard on Eric." Marla quickly cleared up the remainder of the supper dishes and placed them in the dishwasher. "I think he is slowly beginning to change his mind. I'll know more after tomorrow night."

"What's happening then?" Josie waited until Marla left the kitchen before popping another chocolate-covered cherry into her mouth.

"He's taking me to dinner." Marla noticed a dark-brown smudge on Josie's cheek, and reached over to wipe it off. "If you don't stop eating all those sweets, I'm telling Dr. Reynolds."

"You wouldn't rat on your own mother," Josie teased, and Marla realized how little her mother smiled lately. The senselessness of her mother's situation suddenly hit her. Josie was only half a woman without Aaron.

There was only one thing to do. She would find Aaron Westbrook and talk some sense into that man if it was the last thing she ever did.

Josie mumbled good night and headed for her bedroom as Marla grabbed her purse and took off into the frozen night air. In her single-minded determination to see Aaron, she forgot about the new snow and the unplowed roads.

It wasn't until she was already started up the mountain that the folly of her actions hit her.

THIRTEEN

Marla tightened her grip on the steering wheel as she navigated a hairpin curve on the ice-covered roads. She never realized just how fast fifteen miles an hour could be. Or just how icy the roads got after the snow plow smoothed off the powdery snow. At least on the snow she would have been able to garner some traction.

Squinting into the darkness, she tried to locate the fluorescent orange tire marking the turnoff to Aaron's cabin. She had noticed the marker hundreds of times on her way up the mountain when she wasn't looking for it. Now that it was imperative she find it, it was nowhere to be seen.

She pushed her Clint Black tape into the player and hummed along with the soft country music. If Clint couldn't bring a smile to a girl's lips, she must be dead.

Dead! Don't even think about that, she chastised. Wasn't there an old saying about God looking after children and fools? Or was it *animals* and fools? Oh, well, it was about fools anyway and she definitely fit into that category. She could just imagine what Eric would have to say when he found out she had driven up the mountain with these road conditions. He would probably cause an avalanche.

Finally the marker glowed in the beam of her headlights. The turnoff was just ahead and then it was just another mile . . . Another mile! Her muscles were stretched so taut now, she was afraid they might snap. She could only imagine what she would feel like after negotiating that winding dirt road to Aaron's cabin.

She automatically flipped on her right blinker and grinned at the idea of signaling. There hadn't been a sign of another vehicle since she started on this reckless journey. Her car bounced over the slight mound of snow left by the plow and her back tires slid to the right. She steered against the swerve and managed to bring the car under control.

Allowing the car to come to a complete stop, she rested her head on the steering wheel and took a couple of the relaxing breaths she had learned in her Lamaze class. Feeling only marginally better, she urged the little car forward.

After a few useless spins the tires managed to grip the road and inch forward. Actually, this road wasn't too bad, she discovered. Unlike the open highway, the road to Aaron's cabin was protected by thick pine trees, and only a few inches of snow had made it down through the branches to settle on the ground. With the snow providing better traction, Marla felt herself relax for the first time since she had started up the mountain. She leaned back against the seat and rolled her head from side to side trying to relieve the knot of tension in the back of her neck.

Although her speed wasn't over twenty miles an hour, she wasn't prepared for the mule deer to come bounding out of the forest and into the path of her headlights. She screamed and jerked the wheel sharply to the right.

The sideways motion of the car caused it to lose what traction the tires maintained on the road, and Marla found herself slung against the car door as the car spun through the snow, picking up speed with its circular motion.

She tried to fight against the spin but nothing helped. She pumped the brakes. Nothing. Powerless to stop the momentum of the vehicle, she could only pray that her safety belt held.

An icy terror gripped her heart as the car slid off the side of the road and plunged down a steep incline. She heard the grating of branches against the metal of her car as it slid beneath the low-slung branches of an ancient pine tree on the edge of the ravine winding through the mountainside.

Marla heard, more than felt, the crack of her head against the window as the car came to rest against the trunk of the tree. She registered a sharp pain in her hand before giving in to the black void of unconsciousness.

Josie had been pacing the floor since seven o'clock. Where was Marla? She promised to pick Josie up for her appointment at 6:45. Josie called the apartment four times, thinking she might be in the shower. She finally got into her car and drove over to Marla's.

Since Marla was compulsively neat, she had been forced to check the dirty clothes hamper for the black leggings and red sweater Marla had been wearing last night. She checked Marla's reserved parking space and noticed there were no tire tracks on the fresh snow.

Marla never made it home last night. Josie called and canceled her ultrasound appointment and then called Marla's office on the chance she might have phoned there. No one had heard from her.

She checked the hospital, the morgue, and the highway patrol. They hadn't seen her. While this offered her some measure of hope, there was still the slight chance she was out there in a bar ditch somewhere. The police promised to call her if they located Marla or her car.

There was only one person Josie could think of who might want Marla found as badly as she did, and she forced herself to pick up the phone and dial the number. "I'd like to speak to Eric Westbrook, please. It's an emergency."

"May I say who is calling, please?" the desk clerk at the lodge asked.

"Josie Crandall." Josie hoped he wouldn't refuse to talk to her once he found out who was on the other end of the line.

"Josie, what can I do for you?"

The man actually sounded pleasant! "Eric, I'm afraid something has happened to Marla."

Eric shot straight up out of his chair and gripped the edge of his desk. "What's wrong? What happened?"

"I don't know," Josie wailed, giving in to the tears that had been threatening all morning. "She left my house about ten-thirty last night, but she never made it home."

"Where did she go?" Eric busied himself with the papers on his desk, preparing to free the rest of the afternoon.

"I have no idea. She was supposed to pick me up for my doctor's appointment . . ."

"What are you going to the doctor for? Is something wrong?" Eric could feel his heart as it slammed up against his ribs. How much was he supposed to bear?

"Nothing's wrong" Josie hurried to explain. "It's just for a routine checkup, but she didn't show up. I went to her house and she hasn't been there. I've called the police, the hospital . . . Eric, I even called the *morgue*."

A shudder rippled through Eric at the word. "Where are you now?"

"I'm at home. The police said they would call if they found her or her car, but with the weather like it is . ." Josie couldn't bring herself to finish the thought.

"Look, you stay put," Eric ordered. "I'll bring Lanie down to stay with you, and then Aaron and I will go out looking for her."

"Eric?"

"Yes?"

"Thank you," Josie whispered into the phone, and quietly hung it up. She sank down onto her couch and cradled her stomach in her arms. "Oh, little baby, I hope nothing is wrong with your big sister. I can't imagine our life without her."

Eric was a whirlwind of motion. He barely managed to tell his secretary to cancel his appointments before he was sailing down the hall to his apartment.

Lanie was lounging in front of the fireplace, sipping her morning coffee and reading the newspaper when he burst through the door. "What's the matter?"

Eric heard the panic in his sister's voice and cursed himself for not realizing she would be acutely aware of his desperation. He had never been able to hide anything from Lanie. Not his secret hiding place as a child, not his guilt at leaving the grandmothers with her during the winter, not his love for Marla. Especially not that.

Lanie had been surprised to find Eric himself hadn't

quite put that particular label on what he felt for Marla. Once Lanie finally said the words out loud, it had been easier for him to accept. Now that he had accepted it, would he be too late to do anything about it?

"I need you to go to town with me." Eric flung his silk tie on the back of the couch and stripped off the rest of his clothes as he strode across his bedroom to grab his ski suit. "I just got a call from Josie. She hasn't heard from Marla since last night and no one knows where she is. I've got to go find her."

"Give me a minute," Lanie called, running for the guest bedroom she had been using for the past few weeks.

"I'll give you thirty seconds," Eric ordered, and quickly zipped himself into the waterproof jumper and boots.

Lanie was still pulling her sweater over her head as she met him at the door. Her boots were still in her hands and she had to hop down the hall trying to put them on and keep pace with Eric. "Has she tried the police?"

"She tried everywhere." Eric couldn't bring himself to tell Lanie all the places Josie had named. "After I drop you off at her house, I'll head for Aaron's and we'll go look for her."

The ride down the mountain was made in silence, and Josie was waiting for them on the porch when they drove up the driveway. "I haven't heard anything yet. I just called the police again, but no luck."

"I'll find her," Eric promised, and slammed the Blazer into reverse.

Lanie carefully made her way across the snow-covered ground to Josie. "You better get in out of this weather."

"I know, but I want to be out there," Josie gestured toward the mountain, "helping to find her."

"You've got another daughter to think about." Lanie patted Josie's tummy. "Or son. This little one is depending on you more than Marla is right now. Let Eric find her for you."

"I just don't think I could bear it if anything happens to her," Josie cried against Lanie's shoulder.

"Yes, you can." Lanie promised, leading Josie into the house. "But you won't have to. Eric will find her."

Eric squinted at the white countryside desperately trying to locate some change in the landscape that would indicate a car had gone in that direction. Unfortunately, since almost everyone in the area owned a four-wheel-drive vehicle, even the side roads already boasted the crisscross pattern of tire treads.

He inched his way up the mountain behind the snowplow and cursed his brother for not owning a phone. He also swore as soon as he found Marla he was calling the telephone company and having them string a line to his brother's cabin. Aaron always said he didn't want people calling and bugging him while he was working, but this was ridiculous. He could have a private number to be used only in emergencies if he wanted, but a phone number he would have.

Eric fought the urge to pass the huge machine in front of him. He had to keep his head about him if he was to be any help to Marla at all. He searched his heart for a special ache that would tell him if Marla was . . . no longer one of the living. His grandmother once told him the Apache thought it was bad luck to say the word dead. It was much better to say that someone was no longer present. He never held with the superstitions of his heritage, but he wasn't taking any chances. He couldn't bring himself to even think about it. She had to be alive. Hurt he could deal with, Marla's "not being present" was an option that wasn't allowed.

He finally spotted the orange tire up ahead and turned off the main highway. His Blazer easily slid over the mound of snow on the side of the highway and he eased the big truck down the road.

At first he thought his eyes were playing tricks on him. Stopping the Blazer, he got out to take a closer look at the tracks on the road. He hunkered down in the middle of the road and reached his hand out to examine the prints.

Elation soared in his heart as he realized the tracks were not made by Aaron's large pickup but by a much smaller car. Lanie had mentioned that she and Marla had been talking about Aaron when they had gone to dinner the other night. It was possible Marla decided to drive out to Aaron's and have a talk.

If he found her sitting in front of Aaron's fireplace all snug and warm he was going to bend her over his knee and spank her cute little bottom for putting them through all of this worry with such a foolhardy stunt.

He eased the Blazer along the path. He had gone several more yards when he noticed the wide swath of ground that had been uncovered, churning up brown earth to sprinkle over the pristine white snow. His eyes followed the path and he could see the broken branches dangling from the trees lining the path.

It didn't take much detective work to follow the destruction. The marks in the snow were clearly defined, and Eric quickly strode down the incline. The path led to the huge pine tree at the bottom of the hill and his heart stopped. If the car had gained enough momentum during its downhill run, there was every chance it had plummeted off the side of the cliff and into the ravine.

Terror fought for control of his emotions and he forced it down. His heart pounded in his chest and an almost unbearable burning seared his stomach. Terrified of what he might find, Eric half ran, half slid his way down to the edge of the cliff. He peered over into the ravine. His eyes desperately searched the tree-covered area for any sign of a car.

There were no signs that anything had disturbed the natural pattern below him. No sign of fire, no marks on the snow, no broken branches or flashes of metal. He knew the car had to be down there. There was no place else for it to go. He turned to trace his steps back to the Blazer. He would go get Aaron and send him to town for help.

Eric forced his practical mind to make a list of what he would need to make it to the bottom of the ravine. He knew the rescue team would have all the necessary equipment, but he didn't think he would be able to wait until Aaron made it up to the lodge and back down.

He hadn't gone more than a few steps when he heard the music. He cocked his head trying to pick up the sound again. For a moment all he heard was the whistle of the wind as it made its way through the trees around him, but then he heard it again. Clint Black?

He listened, trying to determine where the music was coming from. He walked back up the hill. No, the music faded. He walked a little to his left. No, that was wrong, too. He felt like he was playing a game of I Spy only there was no one there to tell him if he was getting hot or cold.

He carefully edged his way back down toward the edge of the cliff. Yes, the music was definitely louder here. He leaned over the edge and cupped his hand around his mouth. "Marla!"

He heard the faint echo of his panic-tinged voice,

but there was no reply. Only the soft strains of Clint, who no longer sounded like Clint but more like Lurch, the butler on the Addams family. Somebody's battery was dying and he had to find them before the music stopped.

He turned to trace his steps back to where he had first heard the music. Strange, but he could swear that the music was coming from the pine tree. He eased himself under one of the branches that bent down to touch the earth.

"Marla!" His boots slid on the thick muck of mud and pine needles covering the ground as he made his way under the branches. Peering through the windshield, he fought against the nausea rising up in his throat. Marla's head was tilted at an awkward angle and he could see the trail of blood that ran from her forehead down the side of her neck before disappearing under the collar of her red sweater. "Marla!"

He slid across the hood of the car and yanked on the passenger door. It was locked. Eric searched the ground for a rock or a stick, anything he could use to break the back window.

In desperation he finally located a rock large enough to smash the glass and he bashed it against the window. The glass cracked but didn't shatter. He continued slamming the rock against the glass until he was able to get his hand inside and unlock the front door. He felt the broken glass slice into the skin of his wrist and sucked in his breath against the pain but didn't stop. Feeling around until he slid open the lock, he prayed the door hadn't been wedged shut during the wreck.

The door gave with the force of his jerk and he managed to pry it open a few inches. The corner of the door dug into the soft mud, and Eric used his shoulder to wedge the door open enough for him to climb in beside Marla.

"Marla, honey." Eric peeled off his glove and held his fingers against the frozen flesh on Marla's neck. He released the breath he had been holding as he located her pulse. It was weak, but it was there.

He noticed the portable cassette player on the floor board at his feet and switched off the now-moaning Clint Black. Eric had once made fun of Marla's penchant for the good-looking country and western singer, but after this was all over, he was going out and buying every record the man had ever made. "Thanks, Clint."

Eric pulled his jacket off and molded it over Marla. She had been wearing her heavy ski jacket, and he prayed it was enough to have kept her from suffering from hypothermia. "Marla, honey, can you hear me?"

His plea was rewarded with a small, weak moan, and he felt like shouting for joy. "That's a good girl. Listen, I'm going for help."

Another moan. This time clearly distressed.

"I'll be right back, honey." Eric leaned over and kissed the chilly skin of her cheek. "I have to get help."

Eric refused to give in to the desire to carry Marla to the Blazer and the warmth it would provide. From the odd angle of her head, he was afraid she might have a broken neck. If he tried to move her, he would only succeed in making matters worse.

He ran full tilt up the hill and jumped into his Blazer. His tires spun as they sought purchase on the slick ground and he forced his foot to gently press the gas pedal. He left the Blazer running while he bounded up the steps and began beating on the front door. "Aaron, open up!"

Aaron barely unlatched the door when Eric forced

his way in. "Marla's been in an accident. She's hurt and I need you to go down the mountain for help."

"Hurt?" Aaron's sleep-fogged brain tried to make sense of the instructions his brother was yelling at him. "Where is she?"

"She was coming to see you last night and her car slid off the road. I found her down there under that big pine tree." Eric shuffled through the closets until he found what he was looking for. "Is this the warmest blanket you have?"

"What do you mean, she's under the pine tree?" Aaron helped Eric find the wash rags before he destroyed the cabin.

"I'll explain it later. Let's go." Eric strode back to the Blazer and piled the things he had picked up onto the front seat. "You drive."

"I can take my car," Aaron offered, sliding into the Blazer.

"It'll take too long to warm it up," Eric argued. "Marla needs help right away."

Aaron started down the road and stopped when he came to the site where Marla's car had left the road. "When did this happen?"

"Last night sometime." Eric was already out of the vehicle and grabbing at the blankets he had gathered. He had already started down the mountain when he turned around. "Tell them I'm afraid she may have a broken neck."

Aaron blanched visibly at Eric's words, and he didn't bother with good-bye as he headed the Blazer down the road. When Eric had said she was hurt, he envisioned a broken leg or whiplash. A greater sense of urgency overtook him as he realized Eric was talking about life-threatening injuries.

He immediately thought of Josie and what she must

be going through. He tamped down his desire to drive straight to her house and offer her his comfort. He had to get help for Marla first. There would be time to make things right with Josie later.

Eric slid down the incline on his rear end, having given up on trying to keep his balance with his hands full. "I'm coming, honey!"

Marla was in exactly the same position, and he forced himself to check for her pulse again. Still weak.

He slid over next to her and began tucking the blankets over the two of them. Being extremely careful, Eric began to gently rub her hands between his, trying to warm them. "Hang on, honey."

Marla mumbled something and rolled her head over to rest on his shoulder. After his initial terror at feeling her head move, he realized it was a good sign. Surely she wouldn't be able to move her head if her neck was broken.

Holding her as close as possible without taking any chance of causing further injury, Eric began to sing the one Clint Black song he knew. He could have sworn he heard her sigh.

FOURTEEN

Marla turned her head trying to locate that irritating beep. She cracked her eyes open and immediately shut them against the painful glare of the lights. What was that noise? A constant beep-beep that drove her crazy with its monotony.

She tried to swallow but her tongue was twice its normal size and covered with sand paper and her right hand felt encased in lead. In fact, her entire body felt as if it had been mummified. "Mumph."

"Marla, honey?" Her mother called to her and she forced one eye partially open. "Oh, thank God."

"What . . . ?" Marla couldn't get her lips to form the right sounds.

"Shh, honey, don't try to talk just yet," Josie whispered close to her ear, and Marla felt tears of frustration sting her weary eyes and trickle down her cheek. She could feel Josie wiping the side of her face and turned to press her cheek against the comforting hand.

Marla could hear other people enter the room and she tried to place the voices. She immediately recognized Dr. Reynolds when he came to stand next to the bed. "It's about time you woke up, young lady. I've been trying to tell them you were faking just like you used to when you were a little girl."

"That's a secret," Marla managed to croak out.

"Shoot, honey, everybody knows you always got sick just in time to miss your piano recital," Dr. Reynolds joked and pulled his pen light out of his pocket to shine in Marla's dilated eyes. "Looks much better."

Marla tried to talk again, but only managed a creaky gasp.

"Josie, why don't you see if you can't get her to drink a little water." The doctor motioned toward the water pitcher and glass on the night stand. "Better use that straw."

Grateful to finally have something useful to do, Josie busied herself with filling the glass half full and inserting the bendable straw into it. "Here you go."

Marla felt the sharp-edged plastic tube hit her lips and eagerly sucked up the liquid. She almost gagged on the first couple of swallows, but managed to get most of the water down. "Better."

Josie dabbed away the water that had trickled down Marla's chin and offered her another drink. "Not too much at once, honey."

"How's the head feel?" Dr. Reynolds lifted the gauze pad covering the left side of her face.

"How do you think it feels?" Marla relaxed against her pillow and shut her eyes. She was already sinking into oblivion and didn't hear Eric whisper her name.

"Don't worry, son." Dr. Reynolds patted Eric's weary shoulder. "The worst part is over. She will be weak for a while and that bruise is gonna look a whole lot worse before it gets better, but she made perfect sense and that means a lot."

Eric wanted to ask the doctor when Marla would

be able to leave this pale-green room that smelled of disinfectant and death. He had gotten his fill of hospitals and well-meaning nurses during his mother's prolonged illness. He wanted Marla out of here and up on his mountain where he could take care of her.

"Come on Eric." Aaron tugged on his elbow, but Eric refused to budge. "I know you want to be here, but you have got to get some rest. You haven't slept in two days."

"I'll sleep when I know she's all right," Eric promised, more to himself than his brother. He promised Marla he wouldn't leave her and he intended to keep that promise.

He held her in his arms, praying she wouldn't decide to die before the ambulance got there. He cursed himself for every second they spent apart and his own stubborn pride for causing their separation in the first place.

So he begged her to forgive him and promised he wouldn't leave her until she asked him to go. He realized she had been unconscious during the entire conversation, but he said the words out loud. He also told her he loved her. He had said those words out loud, too—over and over and over until Aaron's face had appeared on the other side of the windshield with help.

"If you're going to stay, you might as well take this chair." Josie indicated the lounge chair she had been resting on. "I need to go find something to eat."

Eric nodded as Josie left the room and went in search of Aaron and Lanie. He was tired. He moved the chair closer to the bed and eased himself down onto the dark green Naugahyde. He had to be sure he could hear Marla if she called for him.

Opening her eyes was easier this time. Her head still pounded and she couldn't seem to move her right hand, but the rest of her seemed pain-free. She glanced around the room and noticed several baskets of flowers trying to brighten up the icky green walls.

She scanned the machines around her bed, located the monitor that had irritated her before, and she reached her right hand up so she could better examine the white plaster cast covering it. She vaguely recalled feeling a sharp pain in her hand after she had hit her head.

Why had she hit her head? Being careful not to dislodge the large needle taped to the back of her hand, she reached her unbound hand up to feel the large bandage wrapped around her head. Her memory refused to cooperate when she tried to recall just exactly how she had wound up in a hospital bed with a broken hand and gauze turban. "Was I on a tilt-a-whirl?"

Eric shot straight up in the chair and the footrest came down with a bang. "What?"

Eric seemed to be talking abnormally loud and she winced. "Shh."

Instantly contrite, Eric hovered over her. "I'm right here."

Her heart lurched at the sight of his face etched with worry and fatigue. His hair was sticking up and his clothes looked like they had been slept in. "Are you sick?"

Eric ran a shaky hand over his face and grinned. "Sick with worry. Do you need anything?"

Marla started to shake her head, but remembered the excruciating pain she had felt earlier. "Was I on a tilt-a-whirl?"

"Why do you think that?" Even his extreme exhaustion couldn't dim the brilliance of his smile.

Marla closed her eyes and tried to force the memory.

"All I can remember is spinning around and going up and down."

"Well, you took one hell of a tilt-a-whirl ride." Eric used Marla's description. "You don't remember driving out to Aaron's cabin?"

Marla's eyes widened at the memory. "I went out to talk to him about Mom and a deer ran out in front of me."

"He must have caused you to lose control," Eric deduced. "You were lucky."

Marla indicated her bandaged hand and head. "You call this lucky?"

Eric sobered as he remembered how close Marla had come to winding up at the bottom of the ravine. "When you get out of here, I'll show you just how lucky."

"I'll take your word for it." Marla shuddered. "I never plan on going up that mountain again."

Eric tried to tell himself that she didn't really mean what she was saying. It was perfectly normal for her to want to stay away from the place where she had been hurt. Once she was better, she wouldn't be so sensitive.

Marla noticed the frown on Eric's face but didn't question it. She did, however, wonder how she had wound up in the hospital.

Eric told her about his scouting trip and the Clint Black tape. He left out the part about cradling her in his arms and telling her he loved her. He wanted her love, not her gratitude.

"And you made fun of my Clint Black tape," Marla pointed out.

"Never again." Eric placed his right hand over his heart. "I may even write him a fan letter."

"By the way, was my cassette player hurt?" Marla

asked, remembering how expensive the miniradio had been.

"No, it survived, along with Mr. Black," Eric promised. "All you need is a new set of batteries and you're set."

The doctor came just then, and Marla didn't have the chance to ask any more questions. By the time Dr. Reynolds was through poking and prodding, Eric had slipped away.

Every time Marla woke up she automatically checked the room for Eric, but he hadn't returned since their talk. Most of the time Josie or Lanie was sitting in the green chair next to the bed.

"Marla, can we talk to you?" Josie asked, fussing with Marla's pillows for something to do.

Marla glanced from her mother to Aaron and had a pretty good idea of what they wanted to talk to her about. "So, when's the wedding?"

"Last night." Josie's face lit up and she reached around for Aaron's hand. "Are you sure you don't mind?"

"Of course not," Marla smiled as her mother held her right hand, cast and all. "After all, what do you think I was going to see him for? Magazine subscriptions?"

"That was a damn fool thing to do Marla," Aaron scolded. "I have a good mind to ground you."

"Watch it, buddy." Marla arched her eyebrows. "Besides, you'll have one of your own to deal with pretty soon."

"Yeah," Aaron beamed. "That's why I need the practice. How are you feeling?"

"Much better." Marla didn't protest when Lanie

fluffed the pillows Josie had just bunched under her head.

"Better than what?" Lanie offered a knowing grin.

"Are you happy?" Marla asked as soon as the others left them alone.

"Oh, yes," Josie exclaimed. She leaned over to brush Marla's hair off her face. "After Aaron led the ambulance back up the mountain, he came to get me. He sat with me the whole day and night without ever saying anything about what he was feeling."

"He probably figured you already had enough on your mind," Marla interrupted, no longer surprised at Aaron's sensitivity.

Josie nodded. "As soon as we knew you were going to be all right, he swept me off my feet and carried me to the chapel and proposed all over again. He said he was going to marry me or die trying."

"What about Eric?" Marla hated to put a damper on her mother's festive mood, but it had been his unbending attitude that had caused the problems in the first place.

"I don't know," Josie answered truthfully. "I wish I could say he's changed his mind, but Aaron won't even talk to him about it. He says Eric has enough trouble with his own love life to go messing with anybody else's."

Marla refused to meet Josie's questioning gaze. "Now that you're married, he'll come around."

"I hope so," Josie whispered, and began brushing Marla's hair. "The doctor wouldn't let me bring you any makeup."

"I'll survive," Marla chuckled, and held her hand up to gently press against her bandaged skin. "I don't have many visitors anyway."

"You mean Eric?" Josie asked, handing Marla a tissue.

"I don't understand why he hasn't been here." Marla carefully blew her nose and dabbed at her swollen eyes.

Josie was saved a reply by the arrival of Dr. Reynolds. "Let's see if all this excitement has been too much for you."

Marla dreaded another poking session. "I feel fine."

"Let's see you stand on your head," Dr. Reynolds quipped, taking his flashlight out of his pocket to flash into the brown depths of her eyes.

"I couldn't do that before the accident." Marla held her mouth open for him while he flashed his light down her throat. "Why are you checking my throat?"

"To see if there's anyway to stop that smart mouth of yours." he grabbed Marla's pulse and indicated for the nurse to adjust the bed. "I'm going to do a pelvic to make sure everything is still in place."

Marla grimaced as the nurse helped her ease into the proper position. She counted the tiles on the ceiling to prevent dwelling on her undignified position.

"Looks good, Marla." Dr. Reynolds helped the nurse adjust the bed clothes. "I don't think you're going to have any problems, but I want to keep you here a few more days."

"A few more days!" Marla whined.

"A few more days only if you promise to take a couple of weeks off work and stay off your feet," he ordered. "You don't want to take any chances, do you?"

"I thought you said everything looked good," she argued, hating the thought of two weeks of bedrest.

"Marla, do you want to cause a miscarriage?" the doctor asked her bluntly.

"How can my going back to work cause my mother

to have a miscarriage?'' Marla wailed. Had Dr. Reynolds lost his mind?

Dr. Reynolds told the nurse she could leave before pulling a chair up next to Marla's bed. "Marla, honey, I'm not talking about your mother. I did the ultrasound on her this morning and everything is fine.''

"Then what are you talking about?''

The doctor rested his hand on top of Marla's cast. "I'm talking about your baby. Didn't you know you were pregnant?''

FIFTEEN

"That is just not possible." There had to be some mistake. She would have known if she were carrying Eric's child. She would have known!

"Speaking as the doctor who has examined you since you were four, I can tell you not only is it possible," Dr. Reynolds assured, "it is a fact. Just barely, though. If it weren't for the blood work, we wouldn't have picked up on it yet."

Marla did some quick calculating and nodded. "Maybe four weeks."

Dr. Reynolds was visibly relieved that Marla was no longer questioning his diagnosis. He knew it was very probable Marla had not realized she was pregnant.

"I don't believe this." Marla's chuckle was completely lacking in humor.

"If you can forgive an old man's prying . . ." Dr. Reynolds wrote a few notes on Marla's chart with the gold fountain pen he always carried in his shirt pocket.

Marla could remember him using a similar pen every time he had written out a prescription for her as a child. "Ask away, Doc. I don't have any secrets from you."

"You understand this is strictly personal," he added.

Marla nodded for him to continue. She had a fairly good idea of what he wanted to know.

"If the baby's father is that young man who has camped out at your bedside for the past four days, I think he should be told." Dr. Reynolds gauged her response over the top of his bifocals.

"Do you think he would want to know?"

"Very few men can resist the pull of fatherhood." He smiled at the remembrance of his first child. "I'm betting that he'll be tickled pink—or blue."

"Are you sure the wreck didn't hurt the baby?" Marla cupped her hand over her lower stomach, mimicking a gesture she had seen Josie do a hundred times in the last few weeks.

"As sure as I can be until we do a few more tests. But you *will* stay off your feet?"

Marla nodded and waved as the gray-haired man left her alone with her newfound discovery.

A baby! She was going to have a little Eric. Her smile faltered slightly at the thought of Eric, but even the picture of his frowning countenance couldn't stop the joy welling up inside her. She wanted to tell everyone, but for the first time since her accident she was completely alone.

She stared at the green chair pushed into the corner and pictured Eric sprawled out on it. She didn't know how but she had been aware of his presence even while she had been unconscious. A faded memory of his arms around her, warming her. Of whispered words of love penetrating the fog of her pain. She hoped these things actually had happened and were not merely figments of her imagination.

The doctor said he wanted to run some tests on her first thing in the morning to determine nothing had been damaged. A fear she had never known ate at her heart. A hopeless desperation threatened to drown her with its intensity. Had she killed her unborn child with her foolishness?

It took a bit of maneuvering but she finally managed to grab the phone on the table and drag it onto the bed with her. She searched her still-clouded memory for the number and, cradling the phone against her ear with her cast, she dialed the number.

"Boris? This is Marla Crandall, is Geri there?" Please be there, she prayed. Geri was the only person she could think of who wouldn't feel honor-bound to tell Eric. "Thank you."

"You in trouble, Princess?" Geri barked into the phone.

Marla uttered a sick little chuckle. "Yeah, I guess you could say that."

"What do you need?" Marla heard Geri strike a match and light a cigarette over the phone.

"Right now I just need to talk."

"Shoot."

Marla could picture Geri leaning back in her chair with those army boots propped up on her desk, a cloud of smoke curling around that glorious red hair she would have tied back in a braid.

She could picture her face as she told her about the accident and finally the baby. Concern would darken the green of her eyes and shock would probably cause her to drop the cigarette that hung from her fingers.

A string of expletives blaring through the phone told Marla her assumption had been correct. Geri muttered something about setting the trash can on fire and asked her to hold on. "Now, would you mind repeating that last remark."

"I said, I'm pregnant," Marla enunciated carefully.

"Well, hell, that's great!" Geri exclaimed. "Isn't it?"

"I think so, but I'm not sure how Eric is going to feel about it." Marla felt her stomach tighten at the memory of what had happened when he found out about her mother's pregnancy. "He might think I did it on purpose."

Geri thought about it for a minute. "Yeah, the thought will probably go through his mind. But after he has a chance to get used to the idea, he'll know you didn't."

"Geri, the idea of telling him scares me to death," Marla confessed.

"You want me to tell him?"

"No! I'll do it as soon as the doctor says it's safe for me to drive," Marla promised. "Please don't say anything to him."

"Okay, Princess, I'll give you a while. He's going to know sooner or later, though, and I don't want to see him hurt any more than I do you."

"I'll tell him within the next month." Marla stifled a yawn.

"Sounds like you're ready for a little shut-eye. Call me when you get out of that place." Geri hung up the phone before Marla could say good-bye.

Typical, Marla thought. Geri might be a little rough around the edges, but she had proven herself to be a good friend. Marla would return the favor by keeping her promise to tell Eric about the baby by the end of the month.

Eric turned the key in the lock and was surprised to find the door open. Had he forgotten to lock it that morning? Possibly, since he hadn't been able to keep his mind on much of anything lately.

The first thing that caught his attention was the cinnamon fragrance of the stuff Lanie had put all over the place. Then he noticed the fire and in its flickering light, Marla.

She was sitting on his couch with her arms wrapped around one of the large cushions, sound asleep. Her hair was slightly rumpled and he noticed her lipstick had left a slight smear on the pillow. She was sleeping so peacefully he hated to wake her up, but his curiosity demanded it. He had to know why she was here.

He had given up all hope of ever seeing her again. When Lanie suggested having the entire family to dinner a week after Marla's accident, he thought it might be the perfect opportunity to resume their relationship. Aaron and Josie were blissfully joined in holy wedlock and there wasn't anything standing in their way. He practically skipped down the hallway from his office to the apartment only to find out Marla hadn't felt up to going out. He blamed it on her being afraid of driving back up the mountain.

The next family dinner was held at a restaurant in town. Marla called at the last minute claiming she had to work late. She promised to try and get by, but she hadn't shown up and he had stayed in that stupid restaurant for an hour after everyone else left.

The only time she actually showed up was when Eric hadn't. He had finally drawn the painful conclusion that Marla didn't want him in her life. So he stayed out.

For three long weeks he had made sure she wouldn't have his company forced upon her, and now here she was, sleeping in his living room.

He hunkered down next to the couch and brushed an errant lock of silken hair out of her eyes. Once he touched her he couldn't seem to stop. He allowed his finger to slide down the softness of her cheek and trace the fullness of her mouth.

She twitched her lips against his finger and he grinned, tickling her lips again. "Marla."

"Mmmmm." She stretched and slowly opened her eyes. "Oh, I'm sorry. I didn't mean to fall asleep."

"You must be working too hard." Eric eased himself down on the couch next to her, keeping enough distance so that she wouldn't feel threatened.

Marla shook her head free of the grogginess caused by her nap. That was one thing she had learned about being pregnant. If she was still for more than a few minutes, she was asleep. "I hope you don't mind my coming in and waiting for you?"

"I don't mind." Eric slid over closer and when she didn't stop him, he leaned over and kissed her gently. "It's good to see you."

"I've missed you," Marla whispered against his lips.

"Have you?" Eric brushed her lips once more, gently tracing them with the tip of his tongue.

"Yes." She sighed into his mouth and opened her lips to allow him to deepen the kiss. She hadn't come here for this, but once Eric touched her, she knew she wouldn't deny herself his touch. She couldn't.

"Marla." Eric wrapped his arms around her and crushed her to him. His hands slid over her, desperate in his need to touch her. He pulled her onto his lap so he could cradle her against his desire.

Marla slid her fingers into his hair and held his lips to hers. She could feel her heart pounding as her desire spiraled deep within her. She arched against his seeking hands, whimpering when his hands found her tender flesh.

Eric tightened his arms around her and lifted her with him as he stood. "If we're going to stop, it has to be now."

Marla couldn't find her voice, so she brought her lips

back to his. Eric took this for a yes and strode toward his bedroom. He didn't waste any time teasing her out of her clothes. Later he would take the time to tease and toy with her. Right now the need to bury himself in her and feel her heat pulsing around him was too great.

She helped him rid her of her clothing and found he had somehow managed to divest himself of his own clothes. She relished the feeling of his heated skin sliding down hers as he lifted the covers and lay down beside her.

No words were spoken as they reached for each other and rediscovered their passion. Marla touched, tasted, memorized every part of him, every movement, every feeling.

Eric had never experienced such intensity before, and the magnitude of his feelings for this woman overwhelmed him. He wanted her again almost immediately and the fact he was physically capable of bringing her to fulfillment a second time was a pleasant surprise for both of them.

"I love you," he whispered against the top of her head. He felt himself tense when she didn't immediately reply to his unspoken question. "Marla?"

His only answer was her steady, deep breathing. He smiled a pure male grin at the thought of having worn her out.

The smell of frying bacon brought Marla to her senses in the form of morning sickness. Luckily Eric was in the kitchen tending to the sizzling flesh, so he wasn't witness to her desperate dash across the bedroom.

Shaky from the effort to rid her stomach of—nothing, she wobbled back to the bed and crawled under the covers. Maybe if she lay very still, the bed would stop undulating under her and the churning in her stomach would go away.

Why today of all days did she have to wake up with her first bout of morning sickness? Dr. Reynolds had told her that some women never suffered from the nausea that had dominated the first four months of her mother's pregnancy.

When Marla made it through her first two months without even so much as a belch, she had begun to think she would be one of the lucky ones. She had chosen to forget that Dr. Reynolds also warned her some women didn't experience the malady until later in their gestation period.

She just loved the way Dr. Reynolds talked. He rarely ever came out and said she was pregnant. Most of the time she was "with child" or "expecting." A couple of times he had referred to her "condition" as if it were a disease. Only once had he said she was "in the family way." She supposed he preferred not to use that particular term since he didn't really consider her to be a family.

But she was determined her baby would have a family. This was the end of the twentieth century, children were often raised, quite successfully, in single-parent homes. She had no doubts as to her ability to raise the child herself, but she didn't want to.

She refused to let pride stand in the way of giving her child a loving home with both a mother and father. She knew Eric loved her, just as she knew she could never stop loving him.

"Good morning." Eric's voice took on a husky note as he noticed she was still snuggled under the covers. He looked positively delicious dressed in only his black silk pajama bottoms and a gold-and-black paisley robe. He hadn't bothered to belt the robe, and it hung open to reveal his chest and the hard plane of his stomach. "Ready to eat?"

Marla felt goosebumps rise along her arms at the thought of having to eat. "I'm not very hungry."

"Ah, come see what I made for you." Eric flipped back the comforter and tugged on her foot.

He looked so darned appealing, she couldn't say no. She did manage to snatch his pajama top off the foot of the bed and slip it on. The black silk hung almost to her knees and Eric's smell was woven into the fabric. It did not make her feel nauseous.

Eric had set the dining-room table and there was a fresh bouquet of flowers to replace the dead ones from last night. He pulled out her chair for her and handed her a single red rose. "I'm trying to brush up on my romancing."

"Why?" She held the bud to her nose and brushed the petals across her lips.

"Lanie said I had to work at our relationship." Eric strolled to the kitchen leaving Marla to wonder just exactly how he would define their relationship.

It wouldn't make any difference what he thought they were to each other right now. As soon as breakfast was over and she told him her news, their relationship would take on an entirely new definition.

Marla tried not to smell the bacon when Eric placed the plate in front of her. She tried not to notice the fried chicken embryos. She tried not to think about the cow's milk coating the inside of Eric's mouth as he took a long drink. She tried all these things—and failed.

"Excuse me." She jumped up from the table and ran for the bathroom. If it had been two feet farther away, she wouldn't have made it.

As it was, she didn't have time to shut the door and prevent Eric from following her. "Are you sick?"

"No," she said between bouts. "I'm washing my hair in toilet water to make it shine."

In the split second before Eric recognized her sarcasm he wondered if she actually did wash her hair in toilet water. That or maybe she had lost her mind. "Can I get you anything?"

"Please leave," she cried, and bent over the bowl.

Instead of leaving, Eric opened the linen closet and got a wash rag. She mumbled her thanks as he held it across her forehead. "Do you have the flu or something?"

Marla hated the concern in his voice, hated knowing the concern she heard now could very well be replaced with hard, biting anger when she told him of her condition. "I'm fine, Eric. Could you please go get my clothes?"

Having ascertained she could handle things without him, he left to locate the clothing he had flung across his bedroom last night. A wicked smile curved his lips as he thought about the penchant he and Marla had for tossing their clothes. Must be a rebellious streak in two otherwise extremely neat people.

He managed to locate everything but her bra. Luckily her sweater was large enough that it wouldn't matter. Although he could have sworn she had . . . developed a bit since the last time he had held her close enough to take her measurements.

He laid the clothes on the bathroom vanity and fished a new toothbrush out of the large supply he kept on hand. Marla grabbed the toothbrush and smeared it with paste. He had been a little surprised she hadn't questioned why he kept extra brushes lying around. Of course, she probably didn't feel like an inquisition right now.

He quickly dressed himself and straightened the bed.

His plans for a long, leisurely morning were definitely out. He ought to see if he couldn't get her to have Dr. Reynolds take a look at her.

It had been almost a month since her accident, but Aaron said she hadn't been feeling well since. She had been tired and out of sorts with everyone. He was afraid she might have suffered a more serious head injury than they had been led to believe, but Dr. Reynolds had assured him Marla was behaving in a perfectly normal fashion for a woman in her condition.

He supposed he might be cranky and irritable, too, if he had been forced to stay in the hospital for a week and walk around with his hand in a cast. "Are you okay?"

Marla ran Eric's brush through her hair one more time trying to force it into some style other than "rat's nest." She hadn't been able to find her bra in the clothes Eric had brought into the bathroom, and a quick dash through the bedroom hadn't garnered the scrap of lace, either.

Eric was getting impatient, and she knew the time had come for her to quit hiding in the bedroom. "I'm coming."

Eric met her at the door and helped her onto the couch. She found his solicitude annoying. "Would you stop mollycoddling me? I'm fine."

Eric crossed the room and lifted a multicolored afghan off the back of his chair and brought it to throw over her legs. "You don't get sick when you're fine. I think you should call Dr. Reynolds."

"I already have . . ." Marla began.

"If you knew you were sick, why did you drive all the way up here?" he demanded, clearly thinking she had lost her mind. "If you wanted to see me, all you had to do was call and I would have come to you."

"Eric, please sit down," Marla begged. "I have seen Dr. Reynolds and he promised me everything is fine . . ."

"Fine!" Eric could still picture her sitting on his bathroom floor weak from her illness. The sight of her eyes, wide and dark against her ashen skin, ate at him, and he clenched his teeth to keep from demanding she see another doctor. "I've never heard of throwing up being described as fine."

"It is when you're pregnant," Marla blurted out and slapped her hand over her mouth.

"Sure, maybe if you were pregnant, then I could understand, but—" Eric's eyes widened and he looked as if someone had just punched him in the stomach. "But you're not?"

Marla folded the afghan and laid it on the couch beside her. "Eric, that's what I came up here to tell you."

"When?" His mind was a jumbled mass of gray cells and not one could make sense of what was happening around him.

"Last night." She rose and went to pace in front of the gray ashes in the fireplace. It wasn't quite as soothing as walking in front of a roaring fire, but it would do in a pinch. "I didn't come up here to . . . to . . ." She gestured in the direction of the bedroom.

"To make love." Eric had finally managed to form coherent thoughts again.

"Right," Marla agreed. She chanced a look in his direction and noticed that other than the slightly dazed expression in his eyes, he was responding in a fairly normal manner. "I wanted to tell you about the baby."

"The baby," Eric said. As the initial shock of the situation left him, his mind began to calculate just when the conception would have occurred and how long

Marla would have known about it. "It's been two months!"

When Eric had appeared to be behaving in a rational manner, Marla allowed herself to relax, and his harsh shout startled her. Tears sprang to her eyes and she angrily swiped them away. "I know how long it has been."

"Two months!" he yelled again, and stalked to stare out the dining-room window. "My God, why did you wait so long to tell me?"

"I didn't know until after the accident," Marla cried, and searched through her purse for a tissue. "I should have told you then."

He stared out at the snow-dotted ground and clenched his fists against the rage threatening to spill out and destroy everything in its path. Why had she waited? Why hadn't she told him last night before they made love?

He wanted to pound something. He wanted to make this pain inside him go away. What did she want from him? Why hadn't she come to him, full of joy, and told him as soon as she found out?

He pictured it so clearly in his mind. The way her eyes would have sparkled when she told him. The way he would have kissed her and held her close and promised to be the best daddy in the world. And the best husband.

But she hadn't rushed to him. She had waited until she had no choice. Her body was already changing; he had noticed it last night and put it down to the accident. In a few more weeks she would be forced to wear maternity clothes and then there would be no way to hide it.

She hadn't wanted him to kiss her and hold her close. She didn't want his promise to be the best daddy, the best husband. So what did she want? He turned from the window and slowly crossed the room until he was standing in front of her. There would be no more running. No more hiding. "What do you want from me?"

Recognizing his anger for confusion, she refused to answer in kind. The games were over, this was too important. "I want to know if you love me."

"What?" That was the last thing he expected her to say.

"It's a simple enough question." Folding her arms over her chest, she walked to stand in front of the picture window and stare at the last pink tint of the sky as it deepened to purple.

"I have so many things I need to say to you that I don't know where to begin," he admitted, coming up to place his hands on her shoulders.

Marla heard the pain and uncertainty in his voice and gained courage by it. What was the worst thing that would happen if she told Eric she loved him?

He might laugh in her face. Well, that would be pretty bad, but at least she would be out of this limbo she had existed in for the past few weeks.

"I love you." The words were barely more than a broken whisper, but she had said them and he had heard them.

"You do?" His fingers tightened painfully on her shoulders.

"Yes."

Eric had heard of people bursting with happiness before, but he never actually experienced the phenomenon until that moment. He wrapped her in his arms and held her tightly against him. "I thought I would never hear you say those words to me again."

Marla snuggled against his chest and listened to the

erratic beat of his heart. "I imagine they are nice to hear."

Eric suddenly realized every time he told Marla he loved her, she had been unconscious or asleep. "Not that you would remember, but I have said those very words to you on more than one occasion."

Marla raised her head up to see his eyes. "You have?"

Eric placed a loving kiss on the tip of her nose. "Yes, I have. But I suppose you'd like to hear them again?"

"Only if you mean them," Marla said hesitantly. She still wondered if all this affection was because of the baby.

"Oh, I mean them all right, lady." Eric pulled the envelope out of his jacket and handed it to her. "I do love you. I have for a long time."

"Since when?" Marla opened the letter and quickly scanned the papers inside. "A marriage license?"

"Check the date," he ordered softly. "As for when I fell in love with you; I think it was when you slid into the skis that first day."

"Don't remind me," she murmured, scanning the document in her hand. "This is dated the day after we got back from Vegas."

"Then again it might have been that kiss after you slapped me." He ignored her to let his robe drop to the floor before unbuttoning the shirt Marla wore.

"As soon as that?" She shrugged out of the black pajama top, reveling in Eric's expression as she stood before him in the waning light.

"Had to be." He lifted her into his arms and carried her to the bed.

"I'll buy that." She smiled and ran her finger down the center of his chest.

"But will you buy this?" He played a finger game of his own.

"This?" Marla squeaked, and moved closer to his seeking fingers.

"Us." He nipped on her earlobe and slid her underneath him.

"Is it a good deal?" She opened herself to him and brought him closer.

"Satisfaction guaranteed," he managed to whisper. It was a long time before either one of them could speak again.

EPILOGUE

"Marla, would you mind putting Sammy down for me?" Josie called from the kitchen of her new home. The home Aaron had surprised her with after the birth of their son. Samuel Benjamin Westbrook.

Marla knelt down and somehow managed to lift her four-month-old brother off the floor. It wasn't an easy task considering she was nine and a half months pregnant. "Come on, little guy, Mom says it's naptime."

In no mood to argue, Sammy snuggled into the crook of his big sister's neck and promptly stuck his thumb in his mouth. Josie swore he knew his mother was an old woman and that was why he was such a good baby. Aaron, of course, declared it was his paternal influence. Even Eric took the credit for Sammy's delightful behavior, as well as the infant's angelic looks.

"See you in a little while," Marla whispered to the already yawning baby as she tiptoed out of the nursery and closed the door. Aaron had installed intercoms in every room of the new house so that they wouldn't miss even a tiny hiccup.

"Are you ready for some lunch?" Josie asked as

Marla waddled into the kitchen. "I thought maybe a nice bowl of chili since the weather is starting to cool off."

"Sounds— Oooh!" Marla squealed as a sharp pain cut off her breath. "*Mom!*"

Josie dropped the ladle into the chili pot and hurried to Marla's side. "What's wrong, honey?"

"I think my water just broke." Marla glanced down at the puddle on the floor.

"Looks like a pretty good guess." Josie helped Marla into a chair and gave her a quick hug. "This is it. You sit there while I call the boys."

Marla eased herself into the wooden chair and placed her hands on the tightening muscles of her stomach. It really was happening. After waiting for what seemed like years, she was finally in labor and scared to death. A thousand worries and fears suddenly popped into her head. "Mom?"

Josie hustled into the kitchen with an armload of towels and the cordless phone snuggled against her shoulder. "I can't reach anyone at the office."

"Eric said they were going to walk the trails today," Marla recalled. Positive she still had days before going into labor, she insisted Eric didn't need to stay with her every second. He refused to go to work unless she spent the day with her mother. "There's no telling where they are—" Her words broke off as another sharp pain pierced its way to her backbone. "You'll have to take me."

"Let me call the desk one more time and see if the clerk is back yet." Josie hurried into the nursery to pack a bag for Sammy while dialing the operator.

Marla could hear her mother talking, so she must have reached someone at the lodge. "Call Dr. Reynolds."

"I already have," Josie answered. "He said to come on down the mountain since your water broke."

"I have to get my bag." Marla remembered the bag she had packed for the hospital. It was sitting in the hall closet of the beautiful new home Eric had built for them.

"We are not driving back up just to get your night-gown. You won't need one until after the baby come anyway. They make you wear one of those awful hospital things." Josie hurried back into the kitchen. She had changed clothes and packed Sammy's bag. Handing Marla a pair of old gray sweat pants and a paint-splattered shirt, she rummaged in the refrigerator for extra bottles. "Change into those. You won't win any awards for being the best-dressed woman in the maternity ward, but at least you'll be dry."

"Anything is better than this." It didn't take her long to squeeze into the soft pants and shirt. "I'm ready."

"I got a hold of Blaine at the lodge. He said he would head out right now to find them." Josie wrapped a quilt around the still-sleeping Sammy and hustled them all out the door. "This isn't the way I planned for this to happen, you know."

Marla chuckled at the picture they made. "Me, either."

By the time Josie squealed into the parking lot of the hospital, Marla's contractions were much stronger and closer together. Dr. Reynolds was waiting and made quick work of her examination.

"It won't be too long now, Marla. Where's that husband of yours?" He tugged off his latex gloves and helped her sit up in bed.

"Out on the mountain," she groaned between her clenched teeth.

Josie couldn't find a baby sitter and had to stay in

the waiting room. Whenever the nurses would leave their station she slipped into the birthing room, baby and all, to check on Marla. "Don't worry, honey, he'll be here."

Marla tried to concentrate on her breathing, but it was difficult without Eric's strong reassurance to guide her. "Where is he? I need him."

The nurse came in and shooed Josie back to the waiting room. Marla barely caught Josie's thumbs-up sign before the next contraction hit and she cursed Eric to a life of warts. When the pain became to great for her to bear alone, she called to him. *Loudly.* "Eric!"

"I'm right here, sweetheart." Fighting the panic he felt as he saw her, he ran across the room and grabbed her hand. Bending to kiss her damp cheek, he whispered, "I'm here."

"Where have you been?" she cried as another contraction hit her. "Ow, ow, ow."

"What's the matter? Do you hurt?" Eric felt bile rise in the back of his throat as he watched her fight off the pain. "Are you breathing?"

"Would you shut up!" Marla sat straight up in bed and screamed. *"You did this to me!"*

Eric's face blanched, and he frantically pressed the button for the nurse. "I'm sorry."

"Sorry doesn't cut it, buster," she growled, and fell back on the bed with another contraction. "Eric."

He grabbed her groping hand and tried to remember what they had learned in Lamaze class. He was supposed to take charge, give her gentle commands. He was— "Oh, Nurse, I'm glad you're here. She's in a lot of pain."

The young black woman stared at him as if he had lost his mind. "Most women are, sir. It's a natural part of the birthing process. Didn't you take Lamaze class?"

"All we did was a lot of breathing and massages. They didn't tell me about *this*." Eric was positive the instructor had only said *discomfort*. He remembered her saying the mother would experience a lot of discomfort, but she never said anything about excruciating pain. "Can you make it stop?"

"I'll ask the doctor if he wants to prescribe something for the pain," the nurse promised, and pushed him to the head of the bed. "You stay up there while I check her."

Eric didn't fully comprehend just what the woman was checking for and decided it was one of life's mysteries better left unsolved. Busying himself with wiping a wet rag over Marla's flushed face, he tried to command her to breath.

"I've got to push!" Marla suddenly exclaimed as if she just won the state lottery.

"You just wait a minute," the nurse ordered from her position at the foot of the bed. "Okay, honey, you're a ten. Go for it."

Push! He remembered this part. Maneuvering himself behind Marla, he helped lift her into a sitting position. "Take a deep breath and push, two, three, four, five. Okay, let up."

Marla leaned against his chest and panted from her efforts. "No more babies. This is it."

Eric didn't argue. If they decided on more children, they would adopt. No way would he ever allow her to go through this again.

"Here it comes," Marla warned, and Eric moved into position again.

It seemed to Eric as though Marla had been pushing for several hours, but when Dr. Reynolds finally came into the birthing room he discovered it actually had been a matter of minutes. Having babies was hard work.

"I see you finally got here," Dr. Reynolds said, taking a seat at the foot of the adjustable bed. Eric thought he looked like a baseball catcher.

"Is everything all right?" Eric asked, daring a peek at the action.

"Looks just fine." He reached up and patted Marla on her distended stomach. "A few more pushes and I think we've got it."

At the next contraction Eric helped Marla bear down while keeping his eye on the mirror located in the corner of the room.

"I see the baby," Marla cried, and resumed her pushing.

"Here it is!" Dr. Reynolds declared, and a few seconds later he was laying a squalling baby girl across Marla's much flatter stomach. "She's a dandy."

"Oh, Eric, look at her. She's perfect," Marla whispered, reaching for her daughter. "Eric?"

"Give him a minute, honey," the nurse advised, handing Eric a wet rag.

"I can't believe you did that." He grinned, watching the nurses wash and diaper his little girl.

"I can't believe *we* did this." Marla eagerly took the small bundle from the nurse and gazed down at Eric's face reflected in her daughter. "I want another one."

Only the nurse's quick reflexes kept Eric from hitting his head on the way to the floor when he passed out.

SHARE THE FUN . . .
SHARE YOUR NEW-FOUND TREASURE!!

You don't want to let your new books out of your sight? That's okay. Your friends can get their own. Order below.

No. 44 **DEADLY COINCIDENCE** by Denise Richards
J.D.'s instincts tell him he's not wrong; Laurie's heart says trust him.

No. 119 **a FAMILY AFFAIR** by Denise Richards
Eric had never met a woman like Marla . . . but he loves a good chase.

No. 50 **RENEGADE TEXAN** by Becky Barker
Rane lives only for himself—that is, until he meets Tamara.

No. 51 **RISKY BUSINESS** by Jane Kidwell
Blair goes undercover but finds more than she bargained for with Logan.

No. 52 **CAROLINA COMPROMISE** by Nancy Knight
Richard falls for Dee and the glorious Old South. Can he have both?

No. 53 **GOLDEN GAMBLE** by Patrice Lindsey
The stakes are high! Who has the winning hand—Jessie or Bart?

No. 54 **DAYDREAMS** by Marina Palmieri
Kathy's life is far from a fairy tale. Is Jake her Prince Charming?

No. 55 **A FOREVER MAN** by Sally Falcon
Max is trouble and Sandi wants no part of him. She *must* resist!

No. 56 **A QUESTION OF VIRTUE** by Carolyn Davidson
Neither Sara nor Cal can ignore their almost magical attraction.

No. 57 **BACK IN HIS ARMS** by Becky Barker
Fate takes over when Tara shows up on Rand's doorstep again.

No. 58 **SWEET SEDUCTION** by Allie Jordan
Libby wages war on Will—she'll win his love yet!

No. 59 **13 DAYS OF LUCK** by Lacey Dancer
Author Pippa Weldon finds her real-life hero in Joshua Luck.

No. 60 **SARA'S ANGEL** by Sharon Sala
Sara *must* get to Hawk. He's the only one who can help.

No. 61 **HOME FIELD ADVANTAGE** by Janice Bartlett
Marian shows John there is more to life than just professional sports.

No. 62 **FOR SERVICES RENDERED** by Ann Patrick
Nick's life is in perfect order until he meets Claire!

No. 63 **WHERE THERE'S A WILL** by Leanne Banks
Chelsea goes toe-to-toe with her new, unhappy business partner.

No. 64 **YESTERDAY'S FANTASY** by Pamela Macaluso
Melissa always had a crush on Morgan. Maybe dreams do come true!

No. 65 TO CATCH A LORELEI by Phyllis Houseman
Lorelei sets a trap for Daniel but gets caught in it herself.

No. 66 BACK OF BEYOND by Shirley Faye
Dani and Jesse are forced to face their true feelings for each other.

No. 67 CRYSTAL CLEAR by Cay David
Max could be the end of all Chrystal's dreams . . . or just the beginning!

No. 68 PROMISE OF PARADISE by Karen Lawton Barrett
Gabriel is surprised to find that Eden's beauty is not just skin deep.

No. 69 OCEAN OF DREAMS by Patricia Hagan
Is Jenny just another shipboard romance to Officer Kirk Moen?

No. 70 SUNDAY KIND OF LOVE by Lois Faye Dyer
Trace literally sweeps beautiful, ebony-haired Lily off her feet.

No. 71 ISLAND SECRETS by Darcy Rice
Chad has the power to take away Tucker's hard-earned independence.

Meteor Publishing Corporation
Dept. 1292, P. O. Box 41820, Philadelphia, PA 19101-9828

Please send the books I've indicated below. Check or money order (U.S. Dollars only)—no cash, stamps or C.O.D.s (PA residents, add 6% sales tax). I am enclosing $2.95 plus 75¢ handling fee for *each* book ordered.

Total Amount Enclosed: $_____.

____ No. 44	____ No. 54	____ No. 60	____ No. 66
____ No. 119	____ No. 55	____ No. 61	____ No. 67
____ No. 50	____ No. 56	____ No. 62	____ No. 68
____ No. 51	____ No. 57	____ No. 63	____ No. 69
____ No. 52	____ No. 58	____ No. 64	____ No. 70
____ No. 53	____ No. 59	____ No. 65	____ No. 71

Please Print:
Name _____
Address _____ Apt. No. _____
City/State _____ Zip _____

Allow four to six weeks for delivery. Quantities limited.